Jade wished she had someone to reassure her that she wasn't making a mistake by getting so attached to Nathan.

Too attached. The word *love* lurked just around the corner, she feared.

She'd never been in love with a man, not really. Temporarily infatuated with maybe one or two, but never in love. How could it possibly come to that with Nathan?

How did he feel about her? Oh, he wanted her in the same way she wanted him, but she really didn't know if it went beyond that with him.

She tried to put him out of her mind. He occupied far too much of her thoughts as it was…

Dear Reader,

Welcome to May Special Editions!

Celeste Hamilton's Ashley Grant leads off this selection when she's looking for *A Father for Her Baby* in our **That's My Baby!** slot. Next comes *Wife Most Wanted*, a new **Montana** book from Joan Elliott Pickart. There are seven of these in all and we're sure you'll love returning to Whitehorn. Each story is complete in itself, but those of you who read the original **Montana** books should get extra pleasure from visiting old friends!

Next there's a new **Family Found** novel from the ever-popular, ever-talented Gina Wilkins: *Her Very Own Family*. And Christine Flynn revisits the Whitakers in *Finally His Bride*.

There are also new novels not linked to anything else from Robin Lee Hatcher and Jane Toombs. So whatever your fancy, we should have something to tickle it!

Enjoy!

The Editors

Accidental Parents

JANE TOOMBS

SILHOUETTE
SPECIAL EDITION®

*Silhouette, Silhouette Special Edition and Colophon are
registered trademarks of Harlequin Books S.A., used under licence.*

*First published in Great Britain 2000
Silhouette Books, Eton House, 18-24 Paradise Road,
Richmond, Surrey TW9 1SR*

© Jane Toombs 1999

ISBN 0 373 24247 6

23-0005

*Printed and bound in Spain
by Litografia Rosés S.A., Barcelona*

JANE TOOMBS

was born in California, raised in the upper peninsula of Michigan, and has moved from New York to Nevada as a result of falling in love with the state and a Nevadan. Jane has five children, two stepchildren and seven grandchildren. Her interests include gardening, reading and knitting.

To Elmer, my favourite Nevadan

Chapter One

The potholed road snaked along beside the river that had flooded over it during last winter's storms, damaging the blacktop almost beyond repair. Road crews had filled in only the totally impassable areas, then gone on to deal with other washed-out roads in the county.

Carefully negotiating this barely navigable one with her four-wheel-drive pickup, Jade Adams might have enjoyed the scent of spring sifting though her lowered windows if she hadn't had to concentrate on avoiding the worst spots. No wonder traffic was so sparse.

To her left the river flowed swiftly but so peacefully she could hardly believe the sight of huge boulders and woody debris it had cast up, littering the bank near the road. Beyond the river and also to her right rose the rock walls that had forced the water, over the years, to cut this canyon through them.

The canyon road offered the quickest route be-tween the drill site east of Tourmaline and her home in the Sierras near Lake Tahoe. As she'd expected, the crew had the rig under control and hadn't needed her supervision. Because she was the owner of Northern Nevada Drilling, though, she always checked out new sites. This water well looked to be no problem.

Anticipating the next pothole, Jade slowed for a blind curve. As she eased far enough around it to see what lay beyond, her breath caught. Muttering, "Holy moley," she tromped on the brakes, staring at a white van, its front crumpled against a boulder on the riverbank.

The driver's door was open and Jade could see what looked to be a woman's body hanging partway out. She drove the pickup across the road and pulled onto the bank. When she cut the engine, she saw a red Jeep skid to a stop behind the wrecked van. Jumping out, she hurried to the van, reaching it an instant behind a tall man carrying a black bag.

He pulled a stethoscope from his jacket pocket, then reached inside the van and flicked off the key in the ignition before bending over the woman. Jade breathed a sigh of relief that someone more medi-cally competent than she was going to take charge. She'd learned to handle most emergencies and often had administered first aid when she needed to at drill sites, but she was no doctor, as this man seemed to be.

Satisfied he was tending to the woman, Jade quickly set off flares to warn oncoming traffic of the accident, then peered into the van to see if anyone else was inside. She found herself staring into the frightened brown eyes of a child strapped into the back seat.

She rushed around to the passenger side, slid open the side door and climbed in. "Are you hurt?" she asked the little boy.

He didn't answer. Since she could see no sign of injury, she told herself he must be more scared than hurt, because most of the damage was to the front of the van. Deciding it was safe to move him, she unbuckled the seat belt and lifted him. He wound his arms around her neck and, as she carried him from the van, she marveled at how little he seemed to weigh.

Gazing at him in the late-afternoon sunlight, she noted his face looked vaguely Asian. "Can you tell me your name?" she asked.

His only response was to clutch her tighter.

"Anybody else injured?" the man called to her.

The boy tensed, then wriggled from her arms and began limping as fast as he could toward the river. Jade ran after him, calling, "No! Stop!"

Heart thudding, she caught him before he reached the water. She braced herself for a struggle, but he let her pick him up without even trying to twist away. "You could have drowned," she scolded.

He felt as rigid as a steel drill pipe in her arms. "I'm not going to hurt you," she said softly. "I want to help."

Thinking to shield him from the sight of the injured woman, who might be his mother, she carried the boy toward her truck. He craned his neck to look at the van. The open door concealed the woman, but the man Jade believed to be a doctor, now with a cell phone to his ear, was visible. The boy cringed against her, trembling.

Could he possibly be afraid of the man? Come to think of it, he'd fled right after he heard the man ask if anyone else was hurt. Was his flight caused by the man's voice? Before she thought better of it, Jade called, "Are you really a doctor?"

The man took the phone from his ear and, as he punched in another number, said, "That's what they told me after I passed my Illinois boards. My name's Nathan Walker." Then back went the phone to his ear.

The boy buried his face in her neck, clinging tightly to her. Jade edged into the road to see the license plate on the front of the none-too-new red Jeep. Beneath the snowplow attachment—still on in May?—she noted the personal plate read: BoonDoc.

"Very funny," she muttered. It was a Nevada license plate while the van's was California. If that meant anything.

She watched Nathan Walker put the phone away, then ease the unconscious woman from the van onto the ground so that she lay flat. As he rose, he faced Jade.

"Medicopter's on its way from Reno," he said, walking toward her. "Is the kid hurt?"

"He limps," she said.

"Let's take a look at him."

"He's scared—I think of you. He won't let go of me."

Nathan stared at her. "Afraid of me?"

"My name's Jade Adams," she said, "and I believe you when you say you're a doctor. But I don't know you and so I can't take anything else for granted. This child is even afraid to look at you. I haven't a clue why."

"Neither do I. Tell you what—you keep holding him while I do a quick once-over."

Something about the way he spoke—or maybe it was the way he looked—made her decide to trust him. The boy definitely didn't like Nathan touching him, but he didn't struggle or cry.

"Slightly swollen left ankle," Nathan said when he finished his cursory exam. "Needs to be x-rayed. After the copter picks up…" He paused, glancing from the boy to the woman.

Jade looked at her, too. The woman appeared to be Caucasian, for want of a better term. Not Asian, anyway. Still, she could be the boy's mother.

"The kid doesn't need to be hospitalized," Nathan went on. "No use putting him through any more strange-face, strange-place trauma. For the time being he's better off with us, since he seems to have taken to you. Once she's airlifted, we'll take him to my clinic—it's near Tourmaline."

"In the boondocks."

The left side of his mouth lifted slightly, acknowledging her words.

She'd already noted that he was tall and well built,

wearing his blond hair slightly long. Now she found his eyes were an interesting shade of blue, somewhere between delft and periwinkle. The tiny lines around them put him somewhere in his thirties. Square chin, in need of a shave, and a nose that fit well with his strong cheekbones. Good to look at.

"Did you find any ID for the woman?" she asked, shifting her grip on the boy.

Nathan shook his head. "The kid must be getting heavy. Why don't you buckle him into your truck? It's obvious he won't want to travel in my Jeep, so you'll have to follow me to the clinic. If the deputies don't get here before we leave, they'll know where we are and can talk to us there."

Naturally he'd called the cops, as well as the air ambulance. She always carried her cell phone and would have done the same if she'd been alone.

Nathan watched Jade strap the boy into the passenger seat of her truck before turning back to see how the injured woman was doing. Kneeling beside her, he checked her vitals, not great, but no worse. He'd done all he could for her here; anything more was up to the docs at Washoe Med, once the copter landed there.

Strange not to find any registration or insurance papers in the van—illegal as hell, too. Plus, he hadn't uncovered a handbag of any kind, not even a wallet. Maybe the deputies would discover one when they gave the van a more thorough search.

He stood and glanced toward Jade's truck. She was leaning in the open door, and all he could see was her jean-covered lower legs, ending in heavy boots. The truck had Northern Nevada Drilling lettered on the door. She must work there.

Striking woman—green eyes along with auburn hair, although she didn't have the pale skin usually associated with red hair. Her skin was a warmer color, an enticing one—if he wanted to be enticed.

She straightened and turned toward him. "Aren't they ever going to get here?" she called.

Impatient, he thought, as the distant clack of rotor blades answered her question.

The paramedics had the woman strapped to a stretcher and in the copter in nothing flat. "If she comes to and asks about the boy," Nathan said to them, "let her know he's fine. I'll tell the cops to contact you if they find any info about her."

Stepping back, he felt the rush of wind as the copter rose vertically. As it leveled off to head for Reno, he looked around. No sign yet of any deputies. He waved to Jade, climbed into his Jeep and pulled away. As she followed him in her truck, he nodded approvingly. She might be impatient, but at least she wasn't a tailgater.

As she drove, Jade tried to reassure the boy. "No one will hurt you—I'll make sure they won't. The man who looked at your ankle is a doctor. You don't need to be afraid of him—he wants to help you. When we get to his clinic, he's going to take an X-ray picture of your ankle, but that doesn't hurt."

The boy eyed her warily but said nothing.

It occurred to her that maybe he didn't speak English. Why hadn't she thought of that earlier? "Do you understand what I'm saying to you?" she asked.

Was that an infinitesimal nod? She decided to believe it was. "Good. I told you my name was Jade. Won't you tell me your name?"

"Tim." He spoke so softly she had to strain to hear him.

"Tim. That's a fine name. An honorable name. I'll bet you know how old you are."

Tim didn't say anything.

"You want me to tell you how old I am first? Okay, twenty-nine." And uncomfortably close to thirty, something she didn't care to dwell on.

Tim still didn't speak, but he held up his right hand, fingers spread.

"Five? A good age. I started school when I was five. Do you go to school?"

A tiny negative head shake.

"If you're worried about the lady in the van, they took her to a hospital in that helicopter," Jade told him. "We hope she'll get better there." She hesitated and then asked, "Is she your mother?"

Tim shook his head again.

"Do you know her name?"

No response of any kind.

"Is she someone you know?" Jade persisted with a flick of alarm. Sometimes kids did get stolen by strangers.

He nodded.

So she wasn't a stranger. The woman had looked maybe forty, but that didn't tell Jade anything.

As they exited the canyon, the red Jeep turned onto a narrow side road that was in somewhat better shape than the river road they'd just left. Almost immediately it pulled into a drive leading to a graveled parking lot and stopped. Jade eased her truck up beside the Jeep.

Four big fir trees all but hid the side of the two-story frame building next to the lot. Still, as she got out, she could see the place was far from new—and could use a paint job.

Nathan came up to stand beside her and, as if reading her mind, said, "The town fathers are selling it to me dirt cheap."

In lieu of a comment, Jade raised her eyebrows, then went around to get Tim and lifted him into her arms. Nathan led her along a gravel path to the front where a sign attached to the building read: Tourmaline Rural Clinic. Underneath was Nathan's name and his office hours. She noted he was listed as a family physician.

After he'd unlocked the door and ushered her and the boy inside, she said, "I've discovered his name is Tim and he's five. The injured woman's not his mother, and either he doesn't know her name or won't tell me."

Nathan nodded. "Okay, Tim," he said, "we're going into a room down the hall and I'm going to take a picture of your left ankle—the one that's sore and makes you limp. I'll do my best not to hurt you."

The boy mumbled something that sounded like "Jade."

"Jade's coming with us," Nathan assured him. "She's going to help me."

Once in the room, he told her to sit Tim on the

examining table. "Go ahead and undress him entirely," he said. "I want to make sure he doesn't have any other injuries."

Accustomed to dressing and undressing her young nephew, not to mention her two nieces, Jade started to strip Tim. She hesitated, biting back a shocked gasp when she saw multiple scars and fading bruises over the boy's thighs and buttocks, then went on. Glancing at Nathan, she noticed a muscle twitch in his jaw, but he didn't comment.

He gently urged the boy onto his back, covered him with a small sheet and began to check him over. "Some parts of your body may be sore," he told Tim. "You let me know if any place I touch hurts you and I'll stop right away. Okay?"

Tim reached for Jade's hand, holding tightly through the exam and the X ray of his left ankle. "Get him dressed except for his shoes and socks," Nathan said as he disappeared through the door with the X-ray plates in his hand.

Shock at what she'd seen—obvious evidence of abuse—gave way to anger as Jade carefully put Tim's grubby T-shirt and jeans on again. He wore no undershorts. She'd already noticed the holes in the heels on his socks and in the toe of one of his tennis shoes. Neglect was bad enough, but only a monster would mistreat a child.

By the time Nathan returned to the room, she was fuming.

"He has a healing hairline fracture of one of the ankle bones," he said. "At this point, an elastic bandage ought to be enough."

"Healing?" she repeated. "You mean it's an old fracture?"

Nathan nodded. "Goes along with the scars and bruises, none of which are fresh. Old injuries, probably from abuse."

How could he take it so calmly? He'd spoken without inflection, without any sign of indignation at whomever was responsible for hurting this poor little boy.

"How can you—?" she began, when three sharp rings broke into her beginning tirade.

"Emergency bell—must be the cops," Nathan said as he left the room.

Moments later two deputy sheriffs followed him back into the room, a hefty young male and an attractive, older female. After quick introductions, the man, Deputy Jennings, asked, "This the boy from the accident? What's your name, son?"

Tim scrinched up against Jade, staring at him with wide, frightened eyes, not uttering a sound.

"Here's all we know," Jade said. "His name is Tim, he's five and the injured woman's not his mother." Aware these cops weren't responsible for what had happened to Tim, she reined in her anger, though with some difficulty. "If you feel you must question him, Deputy Danvers should do the asking, because he's afraid of men."

"Any questions can wait," Deputy Danvers said. "Is the boy badly injured, doctor?"

"No."

"In that case we'll bring him back with us," Danvers said.

"No!" Jade cried. "You can't. He'll be terrified."

"Ma'am, we're only following regulations. We have a foster family available for emergencies like this. Tim will be well cared for."

Jade quelled her impulse to flee with Tim, knowing it would do no good. "He's used to me," she said, struggling to keep her tone reasonable. "Why not let me take care of him temporarily?"

"I'm sorry, ma'am, but—" Danvers began.

Nathan cut him off. "You misunderstood me," he said. "Tim isn't badly hurt, but he's not going anywhere with a broken left ankle. I'll have to take care of his injury first. Which will take some time. Once I'm sure the ankle's stabilized, I'll run him in to the sheriff's station myself."

The two deputies looked at each other, then Danvers shrugged and nodded. "Okay, Doc. No problem. We'll need some information about the accident from you and Ms. Adams before we leave, though."

Once the brief questioning was over, Jade and Nathan signed the forms the deputies had filled out. With mixed feelings Jade watched them leave the clinic. Nathan had surprised her by preventing them from taking Tim, but he'd only bought some time, not a permanent solution.

"You said an elastic bandage would do it," she reminded him. "That can't be a complicated procedure."

Removing a tan bandage from a drawer. he began wrapping Tim's ankle. "As you can see, it's not. But this way you can come with me when we bring Tim to the station and they'll probably let you stay with him until the foster family…''

''No, that's not enough.'' Jade looked around, her mind made up. As a business, Northern Nevada Drilling had done its share of local pro bono work, making the Adams name well-known. She'd use the time to call in a favor or two. ''Where's a phone?''

After wrapping Tim's ankle, Nathan led Jade to his office, where she sat in his chair behind the desk with Tim in her lap and picked up the phone. He watched while she punched in one number, then another and another until she finally reached the person she'd been trying to get—a judge named Robinson.

''How are you, John?'' she asked. ''Still cutting deals with the good old boys?''

Nathan raised his eyebrows. Evidently she knew Judge Robinson well enough to slice close to the quick. As he listened to her banter and joke, an unpleasant sense of déjà vu gripped him. She reminded him of Gloria wheeling and dealing, manipulating for all she was worth, out for all she could get and to hell with the other guy.

His three years of marriage to Gloria had made him dislike and mistrust manipulative women. Their bitter divorce had done nothing to change his opinion.

Never mind how attractive Jade Adams was on the outside, or even that her motive wasn't mercenary— this time. He wanted no part of a woman like that. Never again.

Distasteful as he found it, he forced himself to stay and listen to the entire conversation. When she finally set down the phone, he knew she had what she wanted. Judge Robinson was arranging for her to take temporary custody of Tim.

"He heads the children's court," she said. "I knew he'd help me."

Nathan didn't trust himself to speak since he wasn't sure what might come out.

"Tim will be better off with me," she went on. "We've already bonded. He's beginning to trust me. What would he think if I abandoned him? I just couldn't do that—he's had more than his share of abuse and neglect already."

Nathan managed to nod. Tim probably would be all right with Jade. Happier than in some generic foster home. If he didn't think so, he wouldn't let her get away with this. But though she might be the best bet for the boy, it didn't change the way he felt about women like her.

Another thought struck him. "Will it be all right with your husband?" he asked.

"I'm not encumbered with one," she said sharply. "And if I were, why should you think that would make any difference? If you wanted to befriend a helpless child, wouldn't you go ahead and do it, wife or not?"

Touchy, wasn't she? "No wife," he said tersely, imagining Gloria's reaction if he'd ever brought home an abused child. She'd have been on the phone arranging to get rid of the kid before he had the door closed.

Jade took a deep breath, obviously trying to calm

herself. "Where were we? Oh, yes, about the sheriff—John's notifying him."

John? Oh, yeah, the judge. "Bully for him," he muttered under his breath.

Jade frowned. Although she hadn't caught what Nathan said, he sounded angry. At her? That didn't make sense, so she shrugged it off, turning her attention to Tim.

"You're going home with me," she told the boy. "I'll take care of you while your ankle heals."

He gazed at her without speaking.

"You know what's at my house?" she went on. "A black-and-white cat named Hot Shot. Do you like cats?"

Tim blinked, looking confused.

"Well, I guess we'll find out, won't we?" she said, rising with Tim in her arms. "On the way home, how about telling me what you like to eat?"

"Pizza," he said immediately, surprising her. "Hot dogs."

"Guess we can manage that." Glancing at Nathan, she said, "I suppose you'll need to see him again."

"Day after tomorrow," Nathan told her. "Bring him by about noon." He reached a hand toward Tim. "Want to shake on that, cowboy?"

Tim stared from the hand to Nathan's face, looking directly at him for the first time but making no move.

Nathan smiled at him. "Okay, I understand. We need to be friends first, right?"

The smile, Jade noted, was entirely for the boy, none left over for her. A genuine smile, not merely a professional one, it reached Nathan's blue eyes, warming his face and increasing his attractiveness. Whatever she'd done to annoy him, at least he wasn't allowing it to affect his relationship with Tim. And, no, she wasn't imagining things. He was far cooler toward her now than he'd been originally.

Not that it made any difference, she told herself as she carried Tim along the corridor, following Nathan as he opened doors for her, the last being on the passenger side of her pickup. She had no interest in this man other than seeing that he took care of Tim.

Nathan, disgusted with himself, watched her pull out of the parking lot before he went back inside. Why in hell had he told her to bring the boy back in two days? A week or ten days would have been sufficient. He tried to convince himself his slip was due to concern over Tim but failed. The boy's ankle was healing nicely and he had no discernible injuries from the accident.

Nathan's fists clenched as he recalled the evidence of abuse he noted during his exam. Another sick slimebag taking it out on a helpless child. The woman in the van? Impossible to judge at the moment, but if he had even a glimmer of suspicion she was responsible, he'd fight forever to keep Tim away from her.

Provided she lived. He thought she had a fair chance unless her head injury proved to be more extensive than he'd been able to determine.

Entering the kitchen, he filled a mug with cold coffee and shoved it in the microwave, his mind fastening once again on Jade Adams despite his efforts not to think about her. Damn those intriguing green eyes of hers. Not to mention the enticing rest of her. Admit it, he'd told her to return in two days because he badly wanted to see her again.

Which went to prove that fools never learned.

Chapter Two

Jade had stopped at a pizza place in Carson City on the way home, so dusk was settling in by the time she reached the curving road up the mountain toward Incline Village. She switched on her headlights and continued to talk to Tim, as she'd been doing off and on along the way. Not that she got any answers.

"I can't help wondering when you last ate. I don't think I've ever seen a five-year-old boy put away quite so much food in one sitting. You really meant it when you said you liked pizza."

Tim's eyes, she saw, were drooping, reminding her of the way her cat got drowsy after she fed him.

"I hope you and Hot Shot get along," she said. "He dislikes men and doesn't take to everyone else, either. Especially kids, now that I think about it. Not that he'll bite or scratch you—he's not into that. He's exceptionally talented at ignoring people, though. He just looks right through you with those amber eyes of his.

"Speaking of eyes, I wish I could pin down the exact shade of blue Nathan's eyes are. Not cobalt, exactly. Sometimes the blue of the lake is the very same color.

"So what do you think of Dr. Walker? Competent, of course. As well as attractive. Pretty laid-back, though, I'd say. Maybe too much so. This is May, after all. Imagine leaving that snowplow attached to his Jeep when the valley hasn't seen one flake of snow since February."

Glancing at Tim, she saw he was angled to one side, sound asleep.

"Guess my conversation isn't as scintillating as I thought," she said wryly, secretly pleased that the boy felt secure enough with her to sleep. Or maybe he was just too worn-out to stay awake. Or bored with her discussion of Nathan.

Why was she thinking about the man, anyway? He wasn't her type, not at all. How ridiculous to be musing out loud about him.

What she should be worrying about was Tim. He seemed to trust her, but why was he so reluctant to speak? He hadn't said one solitary word on the ride from Tourmaline to Tahoe. He'd even eaten in silence.

When she swung into the village road leading to her street, her headlights picked up the shiny, startled gaze of a mule deer grazing at the verge of the road. Jade slowed, edging past warily—with deer you never knew which way they might decide to leap. Or how many there were. This one fled back into the safety of the pines as she passed.

Tim reminded her of a deer—timid and wary, not knowing what was safe and what wasn't. Had he ever seen a deer?

She'd have to find out—among other, more important information. Such as, if the injured woman wasn't his mother, who was? And where was she? Did he have a father? Where had Tim lived before the accident? With whom? She knew Tim wasn't likely to give her answers to these questions right away, yet it was vital she know.

The injured woman must have the answers, but she was unconscious. When would she come out of it? Soon? Maybe never? Best to remain optimistic about the woman's recovery, Jade told herself.

Reaching her driveway, she pressed the opener and eased the pickup into the garage, although she often left it out. Her brother Zed didn't believe this and teased her about the attention she bestowed on the truck, treating it with far more tender, loving care than his twin gave his foreign sports car. Cars, actually. Talal had more than one stowed here and there about the U.S. And maybe his country, too, for all she knew.

When they saw Tim, her brothers would undoubtedly regard him as another one of her rescued strays. Like Wyatt. But Tim was different. Wyatt had been a teen who needed to find himself. All she'd done was show him the way until, out of the blue, his father had shown up to rescue him. Tim needed to be nurtured. She was determined to do her best to make up for the abuse he'd had to endure.

Luckily she had nothing pressing at the office. The crews were busy, no major problems had erupted and there were orders already in. At the moment she didn't have to go out to assess possibilities to bid on. The time to spend with Tim was there for the taking.

He didn't rouse when she lifted him from the truck and carried him into the house. She hesitated a moment, then decided for this night, at least, she'd put him in the bedroom with the twin beds and sleep in there herself so he wouldn't wake up alone and frightened in a strange room.

Hot Shot appeared in the doorway as she was laying Tim on one of the beds. He jumped up and gave the boy the once-over as she eased off Tim's shoes and socks. The cat seemed to approve, although he regarded the elastic bandage with distaste. Tim, groggy, not entirely awake, seemed unaware of the cat.

Jade rummaged in the closet and found a pair of her nephew Danny's pajamas left behind from the last time he'd slept over. Danny was younger but at least as big as Tim, and the pajamas fit. She tucked Tim in, then bent and kissed his cheek before bundling his clothes together to throw in the washer.

She turned on the night-light and glanced around for Hot Shot before she left the room. To her surprise he was curling himself up at the foot of the boy's bed. Strange. When Danny and her niece Yasmin visited, the cat wouldn't have anything to do with them, usually vanishing until they left.

When she looked in a few minutes later, both boy and cat were sound asleep.

By ten Jade was ready for bed. She undressed in her own room and donned a sleep T-shirt. When she came into Tim's room, he stirred, his eyes opening. He blinked when he saw her. Hot Shot yawned, jumped off the bed and looked up at the boy.

"I gotta go," Tim whispered.

As though he'd known this all along, the cat led the way to the bathroom shared by the two guest rooms. He leaped onto the sink, supervised the proceedings, then returned with them and rejoined the boy in bed.

Tim reached out a tentative hand to touch him. "Hot Shot," he murmured, and was rewarded with a lick of the cat's tongue across his palm.

"I like you," Tim told the cat before he sank back into sleep.

Jade shook her head. Tim had said almost as many words to Hot Shot as he had to her. And voluntarily. Too bad Hot Shot couldn't ask the questions she needed answered. She settled herself in bed, intending to sleep lightly in case Tim woke again, but when she opened her eyes, the room was streaked with light coming through half-closed blinds.

She sat up, looking toward Tim's bed. Empty. Leaping up in alarm, she hurried toward the door, relaxing when she heard childish laughter. The sound came from the kitchen, accompanied by the tiny tinkle of a bell.

Tim was sitting on the floor in front of the refrigerator watching Hot Shot bat the belled toy attached to its door handle—one of his ways of announcing it was time to feed the poor hungry cat.

After breakfast she persuaded Tim to take a bath, trying not to wince at his scars and bruises as she helped him wash. As she rewrapped his injured ankle in the elastic bandage afterward, she vowed fiercely: He'll never go back to his abuser. I won't let that happen, no matter what I have to do to prevent it. He wore the same jeans and T-shirt, freshly washed, but she'd thrown away the socks so the ragged tennis shoes had to go on his bare feet. Number one on her list was new clothes for him.

Shopping in Reno took up the rest of the morning. Jade thought about stopping by Washoe Med to ask about the injured woman, but gave up the idea, aware she'd probably learn nothing. Tomorrow she'd ask Nathan.

Tim was his usual silent self in the department stores, edging closer to her every time a man came near. Even when they entered a toy store, he didn't speak, although his eyes lit up. Jade was reduced to holding up items she thought he might like and, if he nodded, buying whatever it was.

Once they returned home, though, and Hot Shot greeted them, Tim began showing the cat his new toys and telling him all about the trip. She was touched when she realized one of the colorful balls he'd chosen was a gift for Hot Shot.

Late in the morning of the next day, Jade reminded Tim they were going to see Dr. Walker so he could look at the boy's sore ankle.

Tim's face tightened. "It don't hurt no more," he muttered.

Since he still favored that foot, she knew he wasn't telling the truth, but she didn't say so.

"You've already met the doctor," she said. "He didn't hurt you before and he won't hurt you today."

Tim bit his lip. "Can Hot Shot go?"

Although pleased the boy was talking to her, Jade shook her head. "He hates to ride in my truck—or any car—so we have to leave him home. But you can pick one of your toys to take."

Tim chose a picture book about frogs and toads, the only thing he'd actually picked out for himself in the toy store. As he turned the pages, the book made frog sounds, which seemed to fascinate him.

They reached the rural clinic just before twelve. Several cars were in the parking lot and, when they entered, Jade saw patients sitting in the waiting room. When she approached the gray-haired receptionist, the woman smiled at both of them.

"I'll bet this is Tim," she said.

Somewhat to Jade's surprise, Tim nodded.

"I'm Betty Nichols," the woman said. "Doctor wants you to wait in his private quarters on the second floor until he finishes here." She rose and beckoned them to follow her through a door she'd unlocked. "Right up those stairs," she said. "Just make yourselves comfortable."

Tim insisted on climbing the stairs himself rather than being carried. At the top an open door led into a good-sized but sparsely furnished living room. From the corner of the couch a stuffed green frog surveyed the room with black button eyes. Tim made a beeline for it, climbed onto the couch and touched the frog with a tentative finger.

He looked at Jade for approval, and when she nodded, he lifted the frog—a somewhat battered one, she noted—into his arms, hugging it close. Since he hadn't wanted any of the stuffed animals in the toy store, she wondered why he'd chosen this one. True, there'd been no frogs—so that must be the clue. For some reason, frogs appealed to him.

With Tim content for the moment, Jade's curiosity about Nathan got the best of her. She wandered around the room, alert for anything that might reveal what kind of person he was. The few pictures on the walls were desert or mountain scenes, obviously of Nevada.

At the accident scene, when she'd demanded to know if Nathan was really a doctor, he'd mentioned something about Illinois boards. A transplant from the Midwest?

She saw no personal photos in the room, no knick-knacks. The magazines scattered on the coffee table were all related to medicine. Drifting to the stereo unit in a far corner of the room, she picked up a few CDs to check the labels. Country-and-western fan, apparently. She pressed the power button and blinked when she heard music. Mozart, if she wasn't mistaken. Eclectic tastes, the man had. Shutting off the stereo, she glanced at Tim who was now examining the frog intently.

Jade wandered into the kitchen. Basic appliances, all new. She ventured along a short hall leading to a bedroom that contained a king-sized bed, made up neatly, although it hadn't a spread to cover the blanket and sheet.

A framed photo of an older man and woman sat on a chest of drawers. Probably his parents. Next to it was a photo of a pretty but unsmiling young woman who appeared to be in her twenties. Who was she? On close examination, Jade decided she vaguely resembled the older woman in the other picture. Possibly Nathan's sister? Or did she only want to think so?

Jade frowned, annoyed at herself. Why should she care who the woman was? She turned her attention to a small stack of books on the bedside table. A medical text, a popular legal thriller and *Moby Dick*. What was she supposed to deduce from that? If anything.

A sound from the living room made her start, then hurry from the bedroom. Tim, now sitting on the floor with the frog in front of him, was talking softly to it. But not in English. She had no idea what language he used, although she suspected it was Asian.

When he glanced up and saw her, he stopped abruptly, cringing in fear.

"It's all right," she assured him, upset that he might think she'd harm him. "I don't mind. I'm not going to hurt you no matter what words you say."

Seeing his frog book on the couch where he'd left it, she added, "Why don't we sit together and read your book to your new frog friend?"

Which is what they were doing when Nathan walked into the room.

Taken aback by his strange reaction of how right they looked sitting on his couch, he shrugged the feeling away. He couldn't help noticing, though, that Jade's green shirt was the same shade as her eyes— a devastating combination, especially considering how she filled out the shirt. Okay, so she was gorgeous. That didn't make her any less manipulative.

The boy, clean and wearing obviously new clothes, no longer looked scruffy. Okay, so she cared about the kid. Did that change her basic personality? Despite the overreaction of his hormones and his approval of her treatment of Tim, he'd better not lose sight of the fact that Jade was a bad choice for himself.

"I see you've met Frederick Ferdinand Frog," he said.

"Tim took to him right away," Jade said. "Frogs seem to be his thing."

"Okay, cowboy," Nathan said to the boy, "Freddie is all yours. He's been looking for a good home, complains I don't pay enough attention to him."

Tim stared from Nathan to Jade, a question in his dark eyes.

"Dr. Walker means he's giving Freddie the Frog to you," she said. "Just like you gave Hot Shot that ball from the toy store."

"Freddie?" Tim asked.

"That's the frog's name," Nathan said. "My sister, Laura, used to call him Frederick Ferdinand when she owned him. I changed it to Freddie when I acquired him by default after she replaced him with Yonni the blue dragon."

"Oh, you have a sister?" Jade asked.

Why the hell shouldn't he? he thought as he nodded.

Tim stroked the frog's head. Without looking up, he said, "Dragons're supposed to be green like Freddie."

Nathan and Jade looked at each other, eyebrows raised.

"If you say so, cowboy," Nathan agreed. "I'm through downstairs, so what say we take a quick look at your ankle and then have lunch? Heard you like hot dogs. I'll be grilling some in the backyard for anybody who wants one. Or even two."

Tim flashed a quick glance at Jade.

"We didn't expect lunch, but hot dogs sound good to me," she said, pleased Nathan had remembered Tim's food preferences.

Once in the clinic, Nathan replaced the boy's elastic bandage with a new one. Jade picked up the discarded one and rolled it, saying, "I'll wash this and use it as an extra."

"Good idea—waste not, want not, as my grandmother used to say, trying to convince Laura thriftiness was next to cleanliness as a virtue."

"You didn't need convincing?" Jade asked.

"I'm a pack rat. Or used to be."

Noting how his tone had flattened on the last few words, Jade wondered why. Apparently the change hadn't been pleasant.

"Drillers don't throw anything away," she told him. "You never know when an odd length of pipe will come in handy."

"I noticed the drilling sign on your truck. You're connected to the outfit?"

"I run the firm. In the office and in the field." A hint of both pride and challenge tinged her voice.

He smiled. "Explains the work boots you had on when I met you. Ready to eat?"

Tim, who'd hardly flinched at all when Nathan touched him, nodded vigorously.

Nathan led them out the front door and around the house through a gate to the fenced backyard. "I haven't gotten as far as thinking about what to do about landscaping," he said.

Jade saw what he meant. There was a large cottonwood tree in the yard whose shade had discouraged most of the grass. A few scraggly bushes grew near the fence, one a lilac with a few blooms left on it, their sweet perfume carried by the breeze.

An outdoor staircase coming down from the second floor ended in a screened porch. She could see a door in the screen leading to a small stone patio where the grill was set up.

"Be careful, that's hot," Nathan cautioned as Tim edged closer to the grill. "I lit the charcoal before I came to collect you two. Want to help me get the hot dogs, cowboy?"

Tim stared at him apprehensively.

"I'm going to put Jade to work, too," Nathan added. "She's in charge of the buns."

After reassuring himself Jade was following directly behind, Tim trailed Nathan through the screen door to the porch. Inside was a picnic table with two benches. Nathan took hot dogs from a small refrigerator placed against the house wall.

"Freddie can sit on the bench while we tend to the cooking," he said. "Frogs make pretty good supervisors."

Jade smiled at Nathan's nonsense, aware it was gradually disarming Tim. "We can give Freddie the book to take care of," she put in.

Tim's "Okay" made her happy the boy was beginning to feel it was safe to talk to them. Maybe eventually he'd be willing to answer the questions that needed to be asked. Now definitely wasn't the time, because probing might destroy the fragile beginnings of trust.

Nathan's somewhat charred hot dogs were a great success with Tim. Eating one reminded Jade of family barbecues at Zed's ranch, of happy times with her brothers and their wives and children. Next week Zed's wife's brother would be at the ranch, so Zed was planning to have the first outdoor get-together of the year.

Sitting on the bench next to Tim with Nathan across from them, Jade was surprised to realize how much she was enjoying herself. Whatever her reservations about Nathan, he was an easy man to be with.

An impulsive invitation sprang to her lips. "Would you like to come to my brother's ranch in Carson Valley next Saturday for a family barbecue?"

The invitation surprised Nathan, but he took care not to show it. "If I'm able to arrange my schedule so I can get there, I'd like to go."

As he listened to her giving him directions, he kept

wondering why she'd invited him. He hadn't thought he'd made enough of an impression on Jade for her to ask him anywhere, much less to a family gathering. If she were Gloria, there'd be a hidden agenda in her asking, and she'd certainly reminded him of his ex-wife when she made that phone call to the judge. Stay wary, Walker, he advised himself. Don't get to believing she's fascinated by your personality. She wants something, count on it.

"Have you heard how—?" Jade glanced at Tim and stopped.

Nathan knew what the question was. "She's still unconscious but stable."

"No answers yet, then."

He gave her a questioning look, inclining his head toward Tim. Had the boy told her anything more?

"Nothing," she said.

"Jade's got a cat," Tim put in unexpectedly. "His name's Hot Shot and he likes me."

Though Nathan was warmed by this show of acceptance from Tim, he hid his feelings, as he'd done most of his life. His father had never liked displays of emotion. Becoming a doctor and then living with Gloria had reinforced Nathan's tendency to keep how he felt to himself.

"If you've made a friend of a cat," he told the boy, "that means you're an honorable person."

Tim pondered this for a time, then said, "Jade told me my name is hon-or-able. What's it mean?"

"To be honorable is to be a great kid," Nathan said, unsure Tim would be able to cope with anything more profound. "Now you've got three of us—me,

Jade and Hot Shot—who like you and think you're a great kid.''

Tim blinked, glancing uncertainly from him to Jade and back. ''Hon-or-able,'' he repeated, almost under his breath. ''Do big people get to be that?''

''Some do, some don't,'' Nathan said. ''And some try but don't quite make it. How about more potato chips, cowboy?''

Tim nodded, so Nathan poured some chips onto his paper plate. The boy began eating them, frowning a little. Still trying to digest the concept of honorable probably. Not an easy task for many people a lot older than Tim.

The boy had obviously been neglected and abused by those he lived with. Worse than criminal in Nathan's book. Yet kids were resilient—if he became a part of a warm, loving family it wasn't too late for Tim.

He watched as the boy tugged on Jade's shirt-sleeve, saying, ''Maybe Alice tried to be hon-or-able.''

Jade stared at him. ''Alice? The woman in the van you were riding in?''

''Yeah.''

''Know her last name?'' Nathan asked.

Tim shook his head. ''Just Alice.''

''I'm glad you remembered her first name,'' Nathan told him. ''It'll help the doctors who are taking care of her in the hospital.'' He glanced at Jade. ''I'm going in to call Washoe Med and let them know. The last I heard they'd found no ID at all for her.

Even unconscious, patients sometimes respond to hearing their name.''

Jade watched him push open a door and enter the lower level of the house. She'd been annoyed to discover he was even better-looking than she remembered, and it didn't help to realize he moved with an athlete's easy grace.

But a person would swear the man didn't own an emotion. How could he not react positively to Tim's sudden, if tentative, acceptance of him? He knew the boy was afraid of men and was making an exception for him. She'd been ready to jump for joy, but Nathan hadn't so much as smiled.

Not that he wasn't good with the boy. Of course, it could have been his gift of Freddie the Frog that made Tim decide Nathan might be trusted.

Difficult to know where you stood when a man revealed so little of himself. Not that she really cared, in this case.

Turning her attention to Tim, she said, "If you're through eating, we can start cleaning things up for Nathan.''

"He cooks good hot dogs,'' Tim said.

Thus proving the way to a boy's heart, as well as to a man's, was through his stomach?

As he helped her throw the dirty paper plates and napkins into a wastebasket, Tim asked, "Do you like Nathan?''

Jade hesitated before nodding.

"Is he hon-or-able?''

No need to hesitate over that. "Yes, I'd say he's an honorable man.''

"What's a bar-be-cue?"

Tim didn't miss much. "It's a lot like a picnic," she said. "You cook the food outdoors and eat it outdoors."

"Do I get to go?"

"Yes, of course you do. You'll enjoy it just as you did this picnic and you'll get to meet other kids."

"I never been on a ranch."

"My brother has ponies for kids to ride and there's lots of room to run around and make a lot of noise and nobody cares if you do."

"They don't?"

"Not a bit. That's what ranches are for."

"Do the kids at the ranch go to school?"

"Two of them go three mornings a week. But not to what I'd call a real school 'cause they're not five years old yet."

"I'm five and I don't go to no school."

"Would you like to?"

"Not right now. Maybe sometime."

"Every kid has to go to school sometime," she told him. "But we won't worry about it for a while." It gave her a pang to think that Tim might not be with her long enough for her to place him in a school.

"Nathan's coming," Tim announced.

"I swear you have ears like a cat," she said.

Tim beamed, the first genuine smile she'd seen on his face. Apparently he took her words as a real compliment.

A moment later, Nathan pushed the door open and reentered the screened porch.

"We were talking about school," she said.

"You have no way of finding out Tim's immunization record—they'll want that."

She frowned, aware he was right. Chances were the boy hadn't had any of his shots. "I'll manage," she said tersely. Nothing was going to stand in the way of her doing what was best for Tim.

An expression of—could it have been distaste?—flicked across Nathan's face and vanished. No, she must be wrong; she'd done nothing to account for a look like that. Had she?

"We'd best get going," she said briskly. "We've taken up far too much of your day as it is."

Tim picked up his frog. "Freddie's really mine?" he asked.

"An honorable giver never takes back his gift," Nathan told him.

"That's okay, then, 'cause Jade said you're an hon-or-able man. She likes you."

For some ridiculous reason Jade reddened.

Nathan grinned, annoying her.

"Do you like her?" Tim asked.

She noticed Nathan's slight hesitation before he said, "Who wouldn't like Jade?"

Equivocating, the miserable worm. "Plenty of people!" she snapped. "I've never been Ms. Popularity."

Nathan eyed her assessingly. "I wonder why?"

"Because I say what I think." Belatedly she remembered Tim had already told Nathan she liked him. Did she really? Certainly not at this moment.

Chapter Three

Jade awoke on Saturday morning in her own bedroom. Tim seemed content with Hot Shot's company at night, so she'd deserted the guest room, leaving the two of them to share it. She opened the blinds and saw the day was sunny and promising to be warm, typical northern-Nevada May weather. Zed would have a great afternoon and evening for the barbecue.

Would Nathan be there? He'd called two days ago to ask how Tim was doing and to give her an update on Alice, still in a coma. The van she'd been driving had been reported stolen a day before the accident. Investigation of its Sacramento, California, owner showed no known connection to Alice or Tim.

Nathan hadn't mentioned the barbecue, nor had she asked him if he was coming. It would, she'd decided then, make little difference to her one way or the other. The invitation had been offered during one of her impulsive—Zed called them rash—moments, anyway.

The faint tinkle of Hot Shot's come-and-feed-me bell, tied to the refrigerator door, told her where the cat, and probably Tim, were. Barefoot, she padded toward the kitchen, pausing in the archway.

Freddie the Frog was perched on one of the counter stools, ready for breakfast, while Tim sat cross-legged on the floor beside Hot Shot.

"Too bad you can't go to the bar-be-cue," Tim was telling him. "It's 'cause you don't like to ride in a truck. I used to ride on a motorbike when I was real little and I used to get wet. It was somewhere else, I don't remember real good, but it rained a lot and frogs lived there."

The cat stopped batting the toy and regarded him intently, barely glancing at Jade in the doorway.

"Okay, I didn't ride by myself." Tim sounded defensive. "I had to hold on to her."

He still wasn't aware of Jade's presence. She held her breath, listening, trying to figure out where there might be a lot of frogs. Some Asian country in the tropics? And who was the woman he spoke of?

"I like it here. I hope I never go back to *him?*" Tim made it a question, as though puzzled by something.

Hot Shot yawned and stretched, then looked directly at Jade, uttering a feline feed-me command. Tim turned his head and saw her.

"Time to get breakfast for both you guys, I guess," she said, coming into the kitchen.

After they finished eating and she was filling the dishwasher, she said as casually as she could, "I didn't always live in Nevada, you know. I came here when I was a baby. My brother Zed remembers a little bit about living in California, but I don't."

She filled the detergent container and shut the dishwasher door. "It looks like Alice used to live in California—maybe you did, too."

Tim picked up Freddie and hugged him, looking away from her, remaining mute.

Jade sighed. Even the gentlest of probes made him shut down completely. She'd have to be patient.

"So, let's pick out our clothes for the barbecue," she said. "Once we're dressed, we'll have time to walk down to the beach and back before we leave. Okay?"

Tim nodded. He liked the narrow beach along Lake Tahoe, liked going barefoot and wading a few steps into the water, cold as it was.

When she helped him dress, she found the elastic bandage missing. "Gone," he told her when she asked him where it was. "Don't need no bandage."

"We'll have to ask Nathan if you can leave it off," she said as she wound the other clean one around his ankle.

Tim scowled but didn't protest further.

Later she found the missing unrolled bandage hidden behind a stack of newspapers she hadn't yet tied with string for recycling. Since it was Hot Shot's favorite hiding place for odds and ends, she couldn't be sure whether Tim had copied him or whether the cat had actually hidden the bandage.

When they were ready to leave for Zed's ranch, Tim carried Freddie into the truck with him, but once they were off the mountain into Carson Valley, he said, "Maybe Freddie wants to stay in the truck. He might not like bar-be-cues."

"Good idea," she said, realizing how uncertain Tim was about it himself. "Freddie can guard the truck for us while you get to meet Danny and Yasmin and Erin. Just think, you'll be the oldest 'cause you're five."

"I wear Danny's 'jamas to sleep in. Will he get mad?"

"Nope, not a bit."

"Doc gonna be there?"

"You mean Dr. Walker."

"He said I can call him Doc."

"That's okay, then. I don't know if he'll have time to come—doctors are busy people."

"He told me Freddie was mine forever and ever."

"And he meant it. That frog is all yours."

"What if his sister wants Freddie back?"

She hadn't thought Tim was paying attention to the conversation about Nathan's sister, Laura, but the kid didn't miss much. Reaching over, she ruffled his hair. "Laura's grown up now, so she doesn't need Freddie."

Hugging the frog to him, Tim retreated into silence. He didn't speak again until they reached the ranch and parked by the house. "Maybe I can stay in here with Freddie."

"No," she said firmly. "But we can hold hands until you get used to everyone."

Danny came running over as soon as they got out of the truck, shouting and waving a boat. "Tee! Look what I got. Daddy T's gonna help me sail it on the pond later." He slowed as he neared them, his gaze on Tim.

"You can watch," he said to him.

Tim nodded, still clutching Jade's hand.

"You want to see the ponies?" Danny asked.

Tim's grip tightened, so Jade answered for him. "Let's wait until after he meets everyone, okay?"

She started for the backyard with Tim, Danny walking beside the boy and talking a mile a minute. Suddenly Tim stopped, let go of her hand and pointed to the red Jeep with its snowplow attachment turning into the drive. "Doc's coming," he said. "We gotta wait for him."

"Who's Doc?" Danny demanded.

"He fixes up hurt people," Tim said. "He's my friend."

Jade, surprised he'd talked at all, was totally wiped out by his last few words. This from the kid who was afraid of men? Who'd tried to run away from Nathan less than a week ago?

As soon as the Jeep stopped beside her truck, Tim ran over to it. Nathan emerged, grinned at him, reached into the Jeep and brought out a child-sized broad-brimmed hat. He settled it on Tim's head, saying, "Can't be a proper cowboy without the right hat."

Glancing at Jade, he tipped his own hat, a larger

copy of Tim's. "Us newbie Nevadans mean to do our best to fit in, right, cowboy?"

"Right!" Tim beamed at him, touching his own hat with tentative fingers.

"I got a hat like that," Danny said. "I'm gonna go get it." He ran off.

"Do I got to wear that thing on my leg anymore?" Tim asked Nathan.

"If your ankle doesn't hurt without it, no, you don't."

Tim slanted Jade a triumphant look, plopped down on the ground and started taking off his shoe. Nathan smiled ruefully at her.

"I'm glad you were able to come," she said, finding she meant every word.

By the time Tim got the bandage off and was putting his sock back on, Jade saw her brothers advancing toward them.

"A welcoming committee?" Nathan murmured to her.

Taken together, dark-haired, dark-eyed Zed and Talal did look impressive. She was so used to the two of them that she didn't always remember how they affected others. Tim had stopped trying to get his shoe on, staring in disbelief at the two men.

"So this is Tim," Zed said, hunkering down beside the boy. "Let's get that shoe on so you can join the gang."

Without a word, Tim let him do just that, gazing openmouthed from one man to the other.

"My brothers are twins, Tim," Jade said. "Identical twins look almost exactly like each other. The one helping you is Zed, the other is Talal. Guys, this is Nathan Walker.''

Nathan offered his hand to Talal and, when Zed rose, to him.

"I heard there was a new doctor out by Tourmaline." Zed glanced at the Jeep's license plate. "Like it in the boondocks?"

"Beats Chicago," Nathan told him.

"Well, you're welcome out there, I'm sure. Here, too. Glad you could make it."

Danny came dashing up to Tim. "See, my hat's like yours," he said. "I'm a cowboy, too." He tugged at Zed's hand. "Daddy Z, can Tim and me ride the ponies? Yasmin won't care. She's fussing with baby Erin."

"I'll help," Nathan offered. The four of them headed for the corral, leaving Jade and Talal behind.

"You must really like the man," Talal commented.

"If you're referring to Nathan, I barely know him," she said indignantly.

"My dear sister, you haven't invited a man to our family barbecues for going on two years."

"So it was time, right?"

Talal grinned. "If you say so." He glanced at the red Jeep. "They must get a lot of late snow in the boondocks."

Jade bit back a defensive answer, remembering just in time she was being baited. She had no reason to defend Nathan, anyway, she told herself as she picked up Tim's discarded elastic bandage.

"I must say I like his choice of color, though," Talal added. "Come and join the rest of the crew."

"If you help me carry my contribution to the barbecue."

They found Zed's wife, Karen, Talal's wife, Linnea and Karen's brother, Steve, sitting around on the patio watching Yasmin encouraging baby Erin to take a step away from the chair she held on to.

"Jade's doctor friend has arrived," Talal announced.

"He's not mine," Jade corrected automatically, then could have bitten her tongue. Instead of reacting to Talal's teasing, she needed to ignore what he said. "Hi, Steve," she added. "What's with you?"

"Same old, same old," he told her. "I hear you've got yourself a foster child."

"Once I rescued him I could hardly let him be taken by strangers. Did they tell you the entire story?"

Steve shook his head, so she launched into a play-by-play account, finishing with, "Alice is still out of it. The van she was driving was stolen and no one has a clue who she is. Or Tim, either, for that matter. He isn't very communicative."

Steve nodded. "I'll see what I can find out when I fly back home next week."

He wasn't FBI or CIA, but Jade knew from experience that whatever secret Washington agency he worked for got answers quicker than fast. "Thanks," she said.

Looking at Karen, she added, "Your brother ought

to be named Sam, instead of Steve—short for Good Samaritan.''

Karen gave a whoop of laughter. ''Him? He wouldn't know a good deed if it bit him. Steve's just nosy, that's all.''

Steve rolled his eyes, then got up, saying to Talal, ''Past time for us to join the other guys, that's clear.''

When they were out of earshot, Linnea asked, ''What's this doctor like, Jade?''

''A tad too laid-back for my taste,'' Jade told her. ''I need to be challenged.''

''As I recall,'' Karen put in, ''the last challenging type you took up with didn't last through the first round.''

''His problem was trying to turn me into a nice little kitty-cat,'' Jade said. ''He didn't take into consideration that even kittens have claws.''

''And cougars have even bigger claws,'' Karen noted, ''if you don't mind the comparison.''

''Actually I'm flattered. I've always admired them.''

''So Dr. Walker isn't a challenger?'' Linnea asked.

Jade shook her head. ''No way. We don't have any kind of a relationship brewing, and I don't plan on changing that. If we did get involved, in a month or two I'd be walking all over him, and neither of us would enjoy the experience.''

Linnea and Karen glanced at each other, making Jade wonder why. Did they think she liked wiping her feet on men as though they were doormats? Or was it something else?

''But you invited him here,'' Karen said finally.

"You remember I told you poor little Tim showed evidence of abuse? Well, Nathan's gone out of his way to reassure him that not all men are abusive. I thought the invitation was the least I could do."

Deciding the subject definitely needed changing, she called to Talal's and Linnea's daughter, Yasmin. "Hey, bright eyes, how come Tee didn't get a hug?"

"Tee!" Zed's and Karen's daughter, Erin, crowed, holding out her arms to be picked up.

Jade got two hugs, one from each niece, and the conversation turned to the children.

In the corral, the men were applauding Tim and Danny's riding skills. Steve had arrived with Talal, but after being introduced to Nathan, had wandered off by himself.

Pleased with Tim's performance, Nathan said to the boy, "You must have ridden a pony before."

"Before," Tim said. "Back there."

"Back where?" Nathan asked, only to be greeted with silence as Tim shut down. This is deep-seated, he told himself, not just because of the accident. Somewhere, somehow, the kid got the idea that revealing information was dangerous.

A muscle twitched in his jaw as he wondered if maybe Tim had been beaten for it. They hadn't yet invented a name rotten enough for child abusers.

"Good little rider you got there, Nathan," Zed told him. "Somebody taught him right."

Catching an incipient scowl on Danny's face, Nathan realized the younger boy was beginning to resent how everyone's attention was fixed on Tim.

"Danny's no slouch," he told the twins. "One or

both of you turned him into a real cowboy." With
Danny referring to them as Daddy T or Daddy Z, he
wasn't sure which twin was the real father.

"Daddy Z taught me," Danny put in. "Daddy T's
got to go away a lot 'cause he's a prince."

Nathan raised his eyebrows. Talal did have a slight
accent—he hadn't noticed Zed did. But these guys
were twins.

Both of them chuckled, then Talal explained
briefly how they'd been separated as small boys. "I
grew up in Kholi and Zeid here in Nevada. It took
us a while to get together. Since he's more settled
than I, he's raising my son." He glanced at Danny.
"Right, tiger?"

Danny nodded casually. Obviously this was no big
deal to him. "Can me and Tim race?" he asked.

"Maybe the next time he comes to visit," Zed
said, lifting him off the pony. "Time to get honking
with the pit fires or we'll be having a barbecue without any meat."

"Ve-ge-tar-ian," Danny said carefully. "Me and
Yasmin got kids in our school like that. They don't
eat meat. I like meat, don't you, Tim?"

"Yeah. 'Specially hot dogs."

As soon as Nathan lifted Tim down, Danny
grabbed his hand, saying, "Come on, let's go see
Yasmin and Erin. They're my sisters. You got any
sisters?"

"No." Tim gave Nathan a questioning look, saw
his nod and raced off with Danny.

The ankle must really be better, Nathan thought.
It was as good as healed, anyway. He was pleased

the boy had taken to Danny and was beginning to behave like a normal kid.

"Jade seems pretty attached to Tim," Zed said as they started toward the house. "She's got a soft heart under that tough shell."

"Jaida tries to hide it, but she's all heart," Talal put in, giving her name the same slightly different pronunciation he did Zed's. "That makes a woman vulnerable."

Nathan couldn't figure whether they were warning him off or simply trying to explain their sister to him. He decided keeping quiet was the best choice.

"We make her sound like she needs a cardiologist," Zed added, chuckling.

Nathan quelled his impulse to say he was merely a family practitioner. He liked these guys, so no point in sounding like a smart-ass. In his opinion, soft heart or not, Jade seemed well able to take care of herself.

After being introduced to the wives—his medical eye noted Linnea was about five months pregnant—and the little girls, he found himself actively involved in preparations for the cooking and being treated like one of the family. While on one level, it made him feel pleasantly at home, on another, he couldn't help wondering if he was somehow being set up as a prospective husband for Jade.

He tried not to allow his uneasiness at this possibility to affect his enjoyment. While he had no intention of romancing her, much less marrying her—or any woman—he did like her family.

He and Steve were carrying more wood for the fire when Steve asked, "Practiced in Illinois before you came out here, did you? What persuaded you to move to the Wild West?''

Simple curiosity, or was Steve vetting him? Stop being paranoid, he warned himself. "In more ways than one, I got fed up with city life," he said. "When a doctor finds himself thinking of his patients as cases, instead of people, it's time to make a change."

Steve nodded. "If it wasn't for my mountain cabin, I couldn't take my job."

"You have a cabin in the Sierras?"

Without answering the question, Steve said, "Jade asked me to see if my department couldn't come up with something on Alice and Tim. I'll handle that when I'm back in D.C. and call you when we get results."

Not if—when. Interesting. "Thanks," Nathan said. "Both Jade and I are concerned about Tim's past abuse. No way will I let the kid go back to that."

Steve shot him a curious glance.

So he'd been more vehement than usual, so what? He wasn't about to stand aside and allow helpless creatures be abused.

"I'll let you know what I come up with," Steve said. "She's one of a kind, Jade. I met her for the first time when Karen married Zed. Jade and I both laughed at the matchmaking gleams in our respective relatives' eyes. We knew right away we could be friends, but we had enough sense to realize we'd be at each other's throats in less than a week if we got involved. Funny how your nearest and dearest always try to match you up with the wrong people."

"I made my mistake all by myself," Nathan said,

disarmed by Steve's sharing. He rarely talked about his divorce. "Can't blame anyone else."

"Come to that, I did the same," Steve told him. "Makes for extreme wariness when it comes to getting close to any woman again."

"Tell me." He and Steve exchanged understanding looks.

The conversation about relationships and the discussions concerning Jade made for some awkwardness later when he sat next to her at one of the picnic tables while they ate.

"Tim's fitting right in," he said, nodding toward the separate table where every child except Erin was sitting.

"I was hoping he'd feel at home with my nephew and nieces," Jade said. "At first he was afraid to get out of the truck."

Nathan told her about the pony and what Tim said when complimented on his riding ability, finishing with, "But when I asked him where, he clammed up."

"Probably the place with the frogs, wherever that is. I wish you'd heard him talking in that other language to Freddie. Maybe you'd have recognized it."

"I get by in Spanish, but my Asian language ability is nil."

They continued to discuss Tim, she seeming as reluctant as he to get on to any subject that might lead to something personal. Whatever her brothers might have in mind, it was clear Jade had no part in it.

When everyone had finished eating, Nathan tried

to help with the cleaning up but was shooed off by Karen. "I asked Jade to show you the rest of the place," she said. "I'm soliciting opinions on what more should be done with the gazebo and the pond, so keep that in mind."

"Maybe Tim would like to go with us," he said to Jade.

She inclined her head toward where Tim, Yasmin and Danny were hitting croquet balls through the hoops with more enthusiasm than accuracy. "I think not."

Listening to Tim's laughter, he couldn't argue.

Jade showed him the barn and stable first, where he admired the Arabian mare and her handsome two-year-old colt. "Zed's thinking of raising Arabians once Talal can come and go freely in Kholi again so he can choose a couple more choice broodmares for us," she told him.

"Talal's not welcome in Kholi? I gathered he's a prince of some kind."

"He is—it's a political matter. The king's his great-uncle and fond of him, so I imagine it won't be too much longer."

If Zed was his brother and Jade his sister, didn't that make them related to the Kholi king, as well? "Should I address you as Princess?" he asked.

"No!"

"Only Talal has rank, is that it?"

She grimaced. "Actually we do belong to the royal family, the Zohirs, but Zed and I prefer to remain Adamses. Linnea, now, you can call Princess, since she's married to Talal.'' She grinned at him. ''I wouldn't try it, though.''

She bent to pet the calico cat twining around her ankles. As she rose, she said, ''You've seen the corral, so we'll go around to the pond next.''

By the time they reached the gazebo, dusk was settling in. He'd finally gotten used to the fact that the Sierras to the west hid the sun as it went down, making sunset fall earlier than in Chicago. The reward was ''alpine glow,'' a wonderful pink-red that remained in the sky over the mountains until the stars appeared.

Tonight the rising moon was close to full, warm and yellow. As they stood gazing at it, Jade said, ''My brothers are amateur astronomers. If you want to use one of their telescopes...''

''Not until I brush up on what's where,'' Nathan said. ''I like to know what I'm looking at.''

As he spoke, his gaze shifted from the sky to her, looking directly into her eyes. He found he couldn't look away. When he noticed her throat quiver as she swallowed, he knew she must be trapped in the same strange paralysis.

There was no denying she was a beautiful woman. Not pretty—her features were too strong—but beautiful was the right word. In a moment he'd break the grip of what held him motionless; he'd turn away and say something about the barbecue, anything. Just for another moment, though, he satisfied his need to look at her.

What was he looking at, he who always needed to know? A selfish, manipulative woman? A vulnerable woman who was all heart? Both? Neither? How could he tell?

Jade. He was looking at Jade and she was gazing back at him with the same bemusement he felt. Maybe it was a trick of the moonlight, but he saw something in her eyes that drew him to her. Without willing it, scarcely realizing he'd moved, he reached for her, pulled her unresisting into his arms and bent his head until his lips found hers.

Jade welcomed the touch of his lips, only half-aware of her surroundings. Something strange had happened when Nathan looked into her eyes. A feeling of need gripped her, so acute she ached with wanting. Answering his kiss, she slipped her arms around his neck, holding him to her, realizing she fit against him perfectly.

Their kiss blotted out the moon, the night, everything except Nathan. She wished it to last forever, wished she'd never surface or ever have to think again, just feel whatever this was, something she couldn't find words for because it hadn't ever happened to her before.

Chapter Four

Voices intruded into the spell cast by the moon-light—surely it must be the moonlight—bringing Jade back to the reality of where she was and what she was doing. They were at her brother's ranch, she and Nathan, kissing with wild abandon.

Out of the spell or not, it still took effort to move, to extricate herself from his arms and step back, her heart thudding like a bongo drum. Of all the ill-advised actions she'd ever rushed into, this was the prize-winner. She wasn't quite certain how it had happened, but she knew damn well it shouldn't have.

The voices she'd heard she now recognized as Linnea's and Talal's. They were welcome to the moon and the gazebo and the romantic ambience—she'd had more than enough. They weren't visible—the gazebo blocked her vision—but they were headed this way.

She ran her fingers through her shoulder-length hair, wishing she could put her inner self to order as easily. Nathan, standing only a foot or two away, hadn't said a word. She opened her mouth to speak and shut it quickly when Talal's words came clearly to her ears.

"Walk all over him? That doctor's no doormat. All I can say is my muddleheaded sister would make a poor judge of camels."

Unhappily realizing Nathan must be hearing the same words, Jade cleared her throat and, before her brother could unwittingly embarrass her further, called, "Talal? We're over here."

All she could hope for was that Talal's mention of camels might have confused Nathan at least a smidgen. But she doubted it had.

She watched Talal and Linnea amble toward them around the gazebo, trying to come up with something innocuous to say. Talal saved her the trouble.

"Admiring the night sky?" he asked Nathan. He put an arm around Linnea, smiling down at her. "As my favorite astronomer, Omar Khayyám, said, 'Yon rising moon looks for us again.' So we heeded her siren call."

"We're on our way back to the house," Jade put in hastily, "leaving you to commune with the stars and the moon in privacy." Without looking at Nathan, she marched off.

Naturally Linnea had told her husband what Jade had said about Nathan—wives did that sort of thing.

She couldn't blame Linnea. Or Talal, who hadn't known Nathan was within earshot. No, it was her own fault for not keeping her mouth shut. When would she learn?

Even worse was the way she'd lost it when Nathan kissed her, behaving like a moonstruck teenager. Maybe it was just as well he'd overheard Talal. Quite possibly he'd be annoyed enough with her to forget they'd ever met.

After all, he wouldn't need to see Tim again, would he? The boy was the only real connection between her and Nathan. He hadn't said a word since the kiss or since hearing Talal, not one. What was he thinking?

Other guys she'd known would have confronted her about the doormat issue by now. He could be waiting until later so as not to involve any of her relatives in the discussion. He surely wouldn't let it drop without some comment. Unless he really was what she'd accused him of being.

Jade sighed. Doormat or not, that damn kiss was going to take some concentrated forgetting.

Nathan followed Jade toward the house with conflicting emotions. He sure as hell hadn't meant to kiss her. Nor had he expected that one unintended kiss to be potent enough to knock his socks off. Big mistake. Blame it on the romance of moonlight and it still wasn't easy to dismiss.

Talal's overheard remark was even harder to deal with. So Jade thought he was a doormat, did she? Damn the woman. He gritted his teeth, reminded that his ex-wife had probably considered him as tame as

her poodle until he'd shocked the hell out of her by
filing for divorce. Why had he allowed himself to get
even minimally involved with another woman like
her?

One side of his mouth lifted in a bitter smile as
he recalled what Talal had said about Jade's inability
to judge camels. This was one misjudged camel, who
wasn't about to be led into any female's paddock
again.

He figured she expected a confrontation. He'd
learned a long time ago that most of those were like
misfiring rockets, full of sound and fury, then fizzling
out and going nowhere. Occasionally one escalated
into a full-fledged physical fight, which might be
okay if he confronted a man. He'd never hit a woman
in his life and he didn't mean to start now.

He'd liked her brothers and her in-laws—all up-
front except Steve, whose job kept him on the secre-
tive side. Too bad Jade wasn't more like her family.
If she'd called him a wimp to his face, that would
have been up-front. He'd have been mad as hell, but
he could have accepted it more easily than this bad-
mouthing him behind his back.

He was damned if he'd get into any set-to with
her. Ignoring the entire scene was sure to frustrate
her more than him. Nathan nodded. That's how he'd
play it.

Tim came running toward him, croquet mallet still
in hand, with Danny in close pursuit. "Yasmin says
I won!" Tim cried in triumph.

They both came to a halt beside Nathan. "Yeah,

but that's 'cause it's polite to let guests win,'' Danny announced. "My mom says so."

Yasmin, trailing them, arrived. "You just don't like to lose," she informed Danny.

Nathan found a smile for her. "All us men hate to lose," he said. Shifting his gaze to the boys, he added, "We have to learn any one guy can't win all the time."

Jade backtracked to come even with them. "Good for you," she told Tim, extracting the mallet from his grasp. She lifted the hat from Danny's head and tousled his hair. "I'm proud of you for trying to be a good loser. That's a real hard thing to learn."

Danny seemed surprised he'd tried to be a good loser, as well he might be, but at the same time it was obvious her words had mollified him.

"Now that the game's over, let's put the croquet gear away," Jade went on. "Tim and I have to leave pretty soon."

"Can he come back tomorrow?" Danny asked.

"If not, sometime next week for sure," she said.

"I like Tim," Yasmin confided. "He flew on a big airplane from a long way off just like me."

Nathan glanced at Jade and saw the same speculative gleam in her eye that he knew must be in his. Where Tim was concerned they were still on the same wavelength.

"Tim didn't come from Kholi like you, though," Jade said to Yasmin.

Yasmin pursed her mouth. "I know that. He told me it wasn't Kholi."

"Did he tell you the name of where it was?"

Yasmin slanted a glance at Tim and then shrugged. "Just another place."

Nathan wasn't sure whether she was siding with Tim the way kids do or she actually didn't know. One thing was certain—Yasmin wasn't going to reveal any more right now.

The conversation had defused some of the tension between him and Jade. He turned to her and said, "Thanks for inviting me. Your brother has a great spread here. Excuse me while I go and tell him so before I leave." He hunkered down to Tim's level. "I have to go home now, cowboy."

"If I come and see you at the clinic, can we have hot dogs again?" Tim asked.

"We'll see." Nathan had always hated that waffling phrase, but he couldn't promise the boy anything. Tim lived with Jade and he wasn't likely to see her again.

"Maybe when you take another picture of my ankle," Tim persisted.

"Hey, I'd almost forgotten I need one last X ray to make sure it's healed." Nathan's words surprised him. Though it was true he should take one final film in case he was ever sued for malpractice, he hadn't really planned to because it was obvious the boy's ankle was all but healed.

"Just let me know when." Jade's words were clipped.

His nod was as chilly as her voice. He held out his hand to Tim. "A shake to say goodbye, okay?"

Tim took Nathan's hand, shaking it with enthusiasm.

"Me, too," Danny said, offering his hand. "And Yasmin."

Nathan obliged and was turning away when Danny added, "You forgot Tee."

"Tee?"

"Auntie Jade. When I was a baby like Erin, I called her Tee, and now Yasmin and Erin do, too. You can call her that if you want."

"Thanks," Nathan said wryly, "but since she's not my auntie, I'll pass." He had half a mind to forgo the handshake, as well, but he didn't want to upset the kids.

He held out his hand and after a brief hesitation Jade took it. Thinking he might as well go whole hog, he gave her hand a firm squeeze and got one right back in return. Mentally cursing the electric jolt the contact gave him, he dropped her hand and strode away.

Jade watched him go and was in the act of raising the hand he'd shaken to her breasts when she realized what she was doing. Giving a huff of annoyance, she turned to the kids and said, "On the count of three, it'll be time to collect the mallets and balls. One. Two. Three."

Walking slowly after the running children, she muttered, "Okay, so there's *mucho* chemistry. Forget it. Just forget it. Unless you're looking for a major disaster."

From Tim's point of view, the barbecue had been a huge success. During the next few days he talked continually about Danny and Yasmin. He wore the cowboy hat continually, too, hanging it on one of the bed's four posters before he went to sleep. But Jade couldn't get one word out of him about his past.

"Danny and Yasmin go to school," he told her on Wednesday morning. "Maybe I could go with them."

She thought it probably was a good idea. June was nearly here, far too late to enter him in a regular kindergarten, but perhaps the private year-round pre-school they attended could fit him in on their same three-half-days-a-week schedule. She called Karen about it.

"I know they have openings," Karen told her. "But what about Tim's immunization shots? Has he had them?"

"I haven't a clue," Jade admitted. "I could ask him."

"Don't bother. Unless you have a written shot record from a doctor, forget school. Of course, you could always ask Nathan to start Tim's shots. The school might take him if they knew he was in the process of being immunized."

"Thanks." Jade put the phone down and stared at it. So much for never seeing Nathan again. There were other doctors, but she didn't think it would be good for Tim to go to one he didn't know.

"About school," she said to him. "Danny's mother told me you can't go unless you get your immunization shots like Danny and Yasmin did. Do you remember ever having a doctor give you shots?"

Tim stared at her, finally shaking his head. "Does it hurt?" he asked.

"You can ask Danny and Yasmin about their shots when we go to the ranch tomorrow," she said.

When he saw Danny the next day, the first thing out of Tim's mouth was, "When you got those shots for school, did they hurt?"

"Naw," Danny said. "They're nothing."

"It's like you got stuck with a pin," Yasmin put in. "I was scared the first time, but I didn't cry. Erin did, but she's a baby."

Tim looked at Jade. "Okay," he muttered, then ran off with the other two to play.

Jade joined Karen and Linnea on the back patio, where they discussed the house Talal was having built not far away, in the pines near Genoa.

"Zed finally convinced him our place should fit into the surroundings," Linnea said. "So the latest plans feature a log cabin."

"Not just any old Abe Lincoln log cabin, I'll bet," Jade said.

"Naturally not," Karen said with a grin. "You know our Talal. By the way, I called the school and explained Tim's situation. They said if he got started on the immunizations, they'd consider taking him."

"Hand me the phone," Jade said resignedly. She punched in Nathan's clinic number, annoyed with herself because she'd already committed it to memory.

Betty put her through to Nathan and she explained Tim's problem as briefly as she could.

"He ought to be immunized, anyway," Nathan told her. "Bring him in on Saturday around noon."

* * *

On Saturday morning, when Jade caught herself changing her outfit for the second time, she made a face at her mirror image and deliberately donned old jeans and a nondescript T-shirt. She was *not* trying to impress Nathan.

Going to look for Tim, she found him in the laundry room where Hot Shot's food dish was kept. At his feet, Hot Shot was scarfing down his favorite catfish with sauce while Tim murmured to Freddie the Frog, propped on the washer. He spoke words unfamiliar to her in the same singsong pattern she'd heard him use before. Chinese? Japanese? Korean? Vietnamese? She hadn't a clue.

"Telling Freddie where we're going?" she asked, aware he hadn't heard her come in.

Tim started, instantly falling silent.

"Whatever language you were using," she added, "I'm sure Freddie understood perfectly. You can tell by his eyes he's an intelligent frog."

Tim shot her a wary look.

"He probably even knows when you feel good and when you feel bad," she added.

Tim took a deep breath and let it out. "Maybe Laura didn't want to give him to Doc. Maybe she'll ask for him back."

"Why do you keep worrying about Laura? We don't even know her."

"Freddie did."

Jade couldn't find an answer to that one.

They reached the clinic exactly at noon. Once again Betty shunted them upstairs while Nathan finished seeing the patients still in the waiting room.

Tim carried the frog with him, set it on the couch and began wandering around the room much as Jade had done the first time they were here.

"Doc won't care if I look in the other rooms?" he asked.

"We can explore together," she said.

In the bedroom, Tim stared up at the pictures on the dresser. "That lady looks sad," he said, pointing at Laura's picture.

Jade shrugged and led him away, not mentioning Laura's name, hoping Tim wouldn't connect Nathan's sister to the picture. She didn't understand his repeated mention of Laura.

Back in the living room, Tim discovered what was obviously a children's book, a new one, on the coffee table. The picture on the cover showed a boy about his age dressed in a cowboy outfit.

"I think Nathan meant this book for you," she said.

Tim ran his hands over the cover before picking it up. "What's the boy's name?" he asked.

She read the title aloud. "Mike the Maverick." Anticipating the next question, she told him a maverick was a stray, then coaxed him onto the couch with her and Freddie and began to read the book aloud.

Nathan heard her finishing up a story as he opened the door: "...and so Mike knew he'd come home at last."

"And I'm finally home, too," Nathan announced, entering the room.

"We found the cowboy book," she said.

"Jade said it was mine," Tim told him.

"She's right, as usual."

"You gave me my hat, too. And Freddie."

"I did. And it's because you're my friend."

The boy's dark eyes examined him a long moment before he smiled. "Danny's my friend, too. And Yasmin."

"How about Jade?" Nathan asked.

Tim frowned. "She's more like...something else."

Nathan, touched, figured the word Tim wanted to use but couldn't bring himself to do so was "mother."

"Danny says the shots don't hurt," Tim said. "But Yasmin says they do a little bit."

Nathan believed in being honest with kids. "Yasmin's closer to being right. A little bit."

Tim swallowed. "Okay."

"Want to get it over with before we cook the hot dogs?"

"Maybe."

"Sometimes a maybe is a no, sometimes a yes. I'll take yours for a yes."

Jade had hoped they could leave after the shot, but she didn't have the heart to disappoint Tim, especially not after he'd practically called her mother. His stumbling words had brought tears to her eyes.

Downstairs in the clinic, Nathan asked her to stand Tim on the scales, weigh him and measure his height. While she was doing this, with Tim distracted, he readied the immunization shot. After she finished, he had the needle in and out of Tim so quickly the boy barely winced.

"Now that you know what to expect, the next one won't be so bad," he told Tim. "Time to get those hot dogs grilling."

While the cooking was going on, Tim went to explore the yard, leaving Jade alone with Nathan on the screened porch.

"He's acting more like a normal boy every day," she said.

"Kids are resilient, thank God."

More because she wanted to keep the conversation away from what had happened between them than for any other reason, she told him how Tim kept worrying that Laura might want the frog back. "He saw her picture and even though he didn't know the photo was of her, he said 'that lady looks sad,'" she finished.

"Laura..." he began, then stopped and sighed. "You can reassure Tim that Freddie will remain his. I don't think my sister wants any reminders around of her childhood."

Jade waited, her curiosity aroused, but he didn't go on. Whatever Laura's problem was, he didn't intend to share it with her. Which was fine. The fewer confidences they exchanged, the better. Tim was their link, their only link.

Not quite. There was the damn chemistry. He wasn't that close to her, not touching her at all, but she could feel it just the same. She'd been conscious of it from the moment he'd come upstairs.

"Are you going to continue living over the

clinic?'' she asked, trying to distract herself with words.

"For now. Maybe later I'll change my mind. The apartment's handy to the clinic, that's for sure."

"If you got married, though—"

"I don't intend to make that mistake again!" He all but threw the words at her.

So he'd been married before. Unhappily, it seemed. "I didn't mean to hit a nerve," she said.

"You're pretty good at it, though." Anger simmered in his voice.

Jade took offense. Her remark about getting married had been totally innocent. She opened her mouth to say so, but didn't get the chance.

"You can have whatever opinion of me you wish," he snapped. "But why in hell you have to share it with the whole damn world is beyond me."

Jade winced inwardly. He meant the barbecue night. Since she had no possible defense, she said nothing. But irrational as it was, guilt always wound up making her irked at the person who'd caused her to feel guilty, and he was no exception. She tried to tamp down her irritation, but it kept bubbling up.

"Eavesdroppers never hear good of themselves," she muttered.

"I wasn't eavesdropping and you know it."

Knowing he spoke the truth just made her more annoyed with him. She glanced toward the yard, hoping Tim was about to interrupt. But he'd found a ball somewhere and was playing with it at the far end of the yard.

"I prefer not to get into a discussion," she told him. "Let it die a natural death."

He left the grill to tower over her. "In my position, would you?"

She stared at the muscle twitching in his jaw, wondering how soon he'd explode. When it happened, she needed to be on her feet, not scrunched down in a chair. Rising as casually as she could, she told him the truth. "I suppose not." Then, right or wrong, she lost her hold on her temper and boiled over.

"What the hell do you want from me?" she demanded, face-to-face with him. "Hear this and hear it well. I don't grovel."

Glaring down at her, with great difficulty Nathan suppressed an overwhelming urge to grab her shoulders and shake her till she rattled. Violence had no place here. Besides, if he touched her, he might go completely berserk in another way. Never in his life had he been so physically aware of a woman.

What he really wanted to do was fling her onto the floor and take her right here on this damn porch—not an acceptable alternative. He forced himself to step back and take a few deep breaths. The odor of charred meat filled his head.

"I think the hot dogs are done," Jade said, her tone dripping with honeyed sarcasm.

The screen door opened, then slammed shut behind Tim. "Time to eat?" he asked.

As they sat around the table munching on hot dogs and deli potato salad, Tim kept talking between bites. Just as well, Nathan thought. Whether or not his verbosity came from being exposed to other kids, the result was that someone kept the conversation going.

"How come you ain't got a pool, Doc?" he asked. "You got lots of room in your yard. Jade's got a pool inside her house, but we forgot to get a swimsuit for me, so I don't get to swim in it yet."

"I'm not sure I'm going to live above the clinic very long," Nathan said, "so I'll hold off on a pool."

"You mean you're gonna move away?" Tim's obvious distress disturbed Nathan. Was it a good thing for the boy to get attached to him? Sooner or later Tim would have to go back to those he belonged to. But not the abuser—never!

"One of these days I might buy or build a house somewhere around here," he told the boy. "But I'm not leaving Nevada. This is my home."

Tim's relief made him suppress a sigh. He didn't like to think of the boy leaving, either.

"Maybe you can come and swim in Jade's pool till you get one of your own." Tim glanced at Jade for approval.

Nathan knew Jade's smile was forced. "Dr. Walker's busy. He doesn't have very much time to get away."

"He came to Zed's barbecue."

Nathan watched Jade, wondering how she was going to field that one.

"We don't know that he likes to swim or that he'd want to drive all the way up to Incline Village."

She was quick on her feet, all right. "I haven't had a chance to go swimming since I got here," he

said, enjoying the byplay. "Unlike you, Tim, I did
bring my swimsuit with me, though. If an invitation
was extended, who knows, I might decide to try out
Ms. Adams's pool."

Ball's in your court, lady, he thought smugly.

She raised her chin and looked down her nose at
him. "Consider the invitation extended."

The lady had a wicked backhand. Okay, she asked
for it. "Tomorrow's Sunday," he said. "Give me
until noon to take care of any emergencies and I'd
be delighted to accept."

To his satisfaction, Jade blinked. Before she could
say anything, Tim, who'd been looking from one to
the other of them, asked, "Does that mean you're
coming? You guys talk so funny I can't tell."

Nathan nodded. "So you'd better locate a swimsuit."

"Yeah," Tim said, grinning.

On the way home, Jade stopped in Gardnerville to
buy a swimsuit for Tim. Damn the man, anyway. The
last thing she'd ever intended to do was see him so-
cially again, much less invite him to her house. Yet
once Tim got them involved in all this pool nonsense, she'd had no choice.

To refuse to invite Nathan would have confused
and upset Tim, and there was no way she was going
to let that happen. If she was generous, she might
believe Nathan's motives were as honorable as hers,
but she suspected he'd agreed merely to annoy her.
Which he had.

On the way out of the store, a white two-piece suit

caught her eye. She paused to check it out. Not as revealing as a bikini but a long way from modest. She liked the cut. "You need a swimsuit, too?" Tim asked.

Not exactly. On the other hand, the pool chlorine had badly faded her favorite one-piece. "Yes, I do," she said decisively.

Back in the truck with the two swimsuits, Jade told herself firmly that buying the two-piece had nothing to do with Nathan. Summer would bring pool-party invitations by the ton, and it would do Northern Nevada Drilling no good for her to appear in a faded suit. Businesswomen had to take care to look prosperous.

In a swimsuit? Come on, an inner voice whispered, but she cut it off.

"You're sure you know how to swim?" she asked Tim. Although he'd insisted more than once he did, she knew kids tended to exaggerate.

"She called me her little frog," Tim said unexpectedly, "''cause I could swim just like one."

Jade examined his words for clues. *She* again. The same *she* he used to ride behind on a motorbike? Choosing her words carefully, Jade asked, "You don't mean Alice, do you?"

"Naw," he said. "Alice wasn't back there." Before she could ask where that was, something outside caught his attention and he pointed to the right. "Look, there's a red-tailed hawk. Zed's got lots of them near the ranch. Danny says hawks catch mice and eat 'em."

"Hot Shot catches a mouse once in a while," she

said, "But he doesn't eat them—he likes what I feed him better."

"Do you think Doc'll like Hot Shot?"

"Hot Shot won't care one way or the other. In fact, he might not take to Nathan—he doesn't like men. Cats are picky."

"I bet he likes Doc."

Jade hoped the cat would totally ignore him. Too bad Hot Shot wasn't a dog who might nip at Nathan. Or at least growl to show him he was unwelcome.

"Is Doc gonna eat with us tomorrow? Maybe we could have pizza?"

She certainly didn't intend to cook for the man. If she had to feed him, take-out pizza would be the entire menu. And if he had any notion *she* intended to be an entrée, she'd take great pleasure in showing him exactly how wrong he was.

Chapter Five

The next morning after breakfast, Jade clicked the TV to a Reno station for the news. She loaded the dishwasher, decided it looked pretty full and turned it on, not watching the screen or paying close attention to what she was hearing until Tim said excitedly, "They're talking about Alice on the TV."

Thinking he'd merely heard the name Alice, she looked and saw a local newscaster standing in front of Washoe Med.

"...no additional information has been obtained by the authorities about the injured and still-unconscious woman," she was saying. "Alice has no last name. I've been told by a reliable source there was also a small boy in the wrecked van—he apparently escaped injury. My source believes he was placed temporarily in a foster home.

"We're working with the police to obtain a photo of Alice in the hope someone may see her picture on this program and be able to identify her."

"Do they mean me?" Tim asked.

Jade clicked off the TV. "Yes."

"Is my picture gonna be on TV like Alice's?"

She caught back her impulsive *I hope not* and said, "I don't know."

Tim picked up the frog and hugged him, saying, "Freddie doesn't want me to be on TV."

That meant he didn't want to be—making three of them, if she counted Freddie. It wasn't that she didn't wish Tim could be reunited with loving parents. Unfortunately what she'd learned about him so far made her doubt that whoever had been looking after him *was* loving.

He was quiet for the rest of the morning, retreating once again into the safety of silence. Some time later she heard him whispering to Freddie in his other language and decided she'd check out some Asian language books and tapes at the Reno library on Monday. If she could identify what language it was, she'd know what the country "back there" might be.

She had to admit she was now glad Nathan had accepted her reluctant invitation to go swimming. His presence would distract Tim from his brooding and give her someone to share the TV-news invasion with.

When he arrived shortly after one, she greeted him cordially, smiling to herself at his wary expression. What had he expected—a snarling cougar? Tim flung himself at Nathan, hugging his legs.

"Hey, cowboy, I'm glad to see you, too," Nathan said, hunkering down to give him a hug in return. "Got something you want to tell me?"

Was Nathan's sensitivity to nuances something he'd learned practicing medicine? she wondered. Most men she knew, including her brothers, didn't have it.

"Alice was on TV," Tim told him.

Nathan looked at Jade for clarification and she briefed him on the newscast. "Tim's worried his picture might get on TV," she finished.

"Might not happen," Nathan assured the boy. "If it does, we'll just have to deal with what comes up. You're not alone—Jade and I are on your side."

"Don't want *him* to find me," Tim muttered.

"Who do you mean?" Nathan asked. "Who is he?"

Tim shut down.

Time for a switch. "The pool's ready and waiting," Jade said. "The question is, are we?"

Tim brightened and ran off to his bedroom to don his suit, with her calling after him to wait until she got there before going near the pool. She pointed out a bathroom where Nathan could change, then went to put on her two-piece.

The suit fit as well as she remembered from trying it on in the store, but as she examined herself in the mirror, a question surfaced. Just who had she bought the suit for—herself or Nathan? In case the answer was Nathan, she felt tempted to strip it off and go with the old faded one, instead. There was absolutely no reason to try to impress the man, none at all.

Dithering was not her style, so she shook her head and stalked from her room in the white two-piece. What did it matter, after all?

Nathan, with an impatient Tim, waited inside the domed pool enclosure. When Jade appeared, he decided the wait was well worthwhile. The white suit she wore—what there was of it—set off her golden skin, as well as other eye-catching attributes, to perfection.

To rid himself of his instinctive reaction, he made a shallow dive off the side of the pool into the water, heated to a tolerable temperature. When he surfaced, he saw that Tim had jumped in after him and was paddling vigorously over to the other side.

After watching Tim for a bit, Jade walked down the steps into the water and set off in a crawl toward the deep end. Spotting a large orange ball on a lounge chair, Nathan levered himself out and tossed the ball to Tim before leaping back in.

Soon the three of them were flipping the ball back and forth. "Any rules?" Jade called.

"Nope," he said. "None. Orange balls don't like rules, do they, cowboy?"

Tim, grinning, shook his head.

After a time, Nathan noticed a large black-and-white cat perched on a plant table well back from the edge of the pool. From the animal's supercilious gaze it was clear he thought humans were out of their minds to splash around in that nasty wet stuff.

"Who's that?" he asked Tim, pointing.

"He's my friend Hot Shot. He's real smart."

"Picky, too," Jade said. "He likes very few people."

Taking her words as a challenge, Nathan climbed out of the pool, grabbed a towel and eased into a chair near the plant table, careful to pay no attention to the cat. It wasn't long before curiosity drove Hot Shot off the table and over to check out the stranger.

Nathan casually let his hand dangle down within the cat's reach. Cautiously Hot Shot eased closer and sniffed at his fingers. Once the cat was satisfied, Nathan rose slowly and made his way back to the pool. Contact had been established. Now it was up to Hot Shot.

Before he dove back in, a chime sounded.

"The doorbell," Jade muttered.

"I can get it if you like," Nathan offered.

She shrugged, which he took as an affirmative and, towel draped over his shoulders, made his way to the front door. Through the small windows on one side, he saw a uniformed officer on the step and opened the door.

"Deputy Haines," the officer said. "I'm looking for a Ms. Jade Adams. Is she in?"

"In the pool, at the moment," Nathan told him. "Why don't you come in and wait while I tell her you're here."

By the time he reached the pool enclosure, Jade was toweling herself off. "Who was it?" she asked.

"Deputy Sheriff Haines to see you. He's waiting in the living room."

Jade frowned. "Watch Tim, will you?" she said as she shrugged on a terry-cloth robe.

When she left, Nathan motioned to Tim to get out of the pool. "We'll get dressed," he said. "If things go okay, maybe we can have another swim later."

Tim made a face but let himself be ushered from the pool area into the main house where he disappeared into a bedroom. In the bathroom assigned to him, Nathan found the cat sitting on the T-shirt he'd left on the counter.

"Guard cat, are you?" he asked as he shucked his suit and hastily threw on his clothes. In view of that newscast, he wanted to get out there and back up Jade. The cop might be there on another matter entirely, but he didn't think so.

When he reached for the T-shirt, Hot Shot jumped down and Nathan opened the bathroom door to let him out. On the way to the living room, he detoured to Tim's room, finding the cat had gotten there ahead of him. "Stay in here with Hot Shot, okay?" he told Tim. "I'll come back and get you in a little bit."

Tim stared at him wide-eyed. "Is it *him?*" he whispered.

"No. Jade's talking to a policeman, that's all, and I need to hear what he has to stay. It's better if you stay in your room while we talk to Deputy Haines. Understand?"

Tim nodded and lifted Freddie from the bed, hugging him close.

Nathan strode into the living room as the deputy was saying, "I really do need to speak to the boy, Ms. Adams."

Jade, obviously not only upset but angry, shook her head. "Didn't you hear what I said? He isn't—"

Nathan cut in. "If you're referring to the boy Ms. Adams is fostering, my name is Dr. Walker and I'm the child's physician. Do you have any questions you'd like to address to me?"

"I've been sent to question the boy about the van he was riding in when the accident occurred. We need to know if he—"

Nathan thought quickly. "I'm sorry, but the child is extremely disturbed and under the care of a psychiatrist. I'd need to check with her before I can allow anyone to talk to the boy. Perhaps you could arrange to ask your questions through her—if she feels that approach wouldn't harm her patient."

"If that's the case, I'll need to know the psychiatrist's name."

"Certainly. She's Dr. Gertrude Severin, practicing in Tourmaline, as I do. You'll find her office number in the phone book. Mine, too, should you need it."

"And the boy's name?" the deputy persisted.

"All any of us know is his first name—Tim. As I explained, he suffered a severe traumatic disturbance."

Deputy Haines put away his notebook, wished them a good day and left.

After closing the door behind him, Jade swung around to stare at Nathan. "What's all this about?"

"I'll explain later," he said, thumbing through his wallet. "Where's your phone?"

She showed him. Extracting a card from the wallet, he punched in a private number, breathing a sigh of relief when he heard Gertrude Severin's voice on the other end.

''Gert, this is Nathan,'' he said. ''Glad I caught you home. I need you to cover my ass.''

Jade shook her head as she listened to Nathan explaining the problem to someone named Gert, presumably the psychiatrist he'd claimed was seeing Tim. He'd been so convincing talking to the deputy that she'd begun to believe he actually had discussed Tim with this woman. But it was clear he hadn't until this phone call.

Leaving him to his persuasion, she checked on Tim and found him huddled on his bed with Hot Shot and Freddie. After reassuring him everything was all right, she hurried to her room and flung on her clothes.

When she returned to the living room, Nathan was just putting down the phone. ''Gert's going to cover for us,'' he told her. ''I owe her big-time.''

''You are one devious man,'' she said.

He gave her a very odd look.

''Well,'' she said, ''you had me, right along with the cop, convinced a shrink was involved—even though I knew Tim had never been to her.''

''Gert's a good gal.''

Jade brushed away the question of just how friendly he and Gert were. What difference did it make to her?

''Tim's scared,'' she said. ''I hope this thing doesn't escalate. For now, though, since you're so effective on the phone, why don't you call in a pizza order while I try to convince him everything's all right? Just punch in six—that's the pizza number.''

She started out, pausing to add, "Tim likes anchovies."

Nathan happened to hate them, but he placed the order with anchovies. *Escalate* was a mild word for what he feared might happen. He could stall the cops, but what about the media? He hoped Alice's plight would turn out to be of only temporary local interest, but there was a chance the story might be picked up by one of the networks and go nationwide. Then how could he and Jade protect the boy?

The arrival of the pizza cheered Tim considerably. Hot Shot, Nathan discovered, was more than happy to eat the anchovies he picked off his slices, so everyone was satisfied.

"We don't usually feed the cat at the table," Jade said. But her tone was nonconfrontational. Apparently the threat to the boy had brought them together in one camp—Tim's.

"I'll remember that for next time," Nathan assured her.

She didn't challenge the "next time," either. His mental picture of her in the white swimsuit forced him to acknowledge it wasn't entirely for Tim's sake that he wanted there to be a next time.

After they finished eating, Tim reminded her about the Disney movie she'd promised he could watch. They left him lying on his stomach in front of the family-room TV, chin propped on Freddie, Hot Shot curled up next to him.

As Jade led Nathan into the living room, he scotched his half-formed notion that he'd enjoy lounging by the pool with her, lights off, so the night sky was visible. The episode by Zed's gazebo had been warning enough. If he didn't want to get any more involved with Jade than he was already, night skies were best left alone.

He settled onto a white wicker couch, hoping despite his reservations she'd sit next to him. She chose a nearby chair, instead.

"I didn't get a chance to tell you what that deputy wanted to ask Tim." she said. "When they checked the van thoroughly, they found some marijuana. Not much, but you know Nevada law. Possession of even a little means a felony charge. So they thought they'd question Tim about it. Imagine! What could a five-year-old possibly know about that?"

Nathan, with his eye-opening past experience at Cook County Hospital in Chicago, could have told her horror stories about drugs and small children but chose not to.

"The van was stolen—possibly the stuff belonged to the owner, rather than Alice," he said.

"I reminded the deputy the van had been stolen in California, but he insisted he had to talk to Tim, anyway. Thank heaven you threw Gert at him."

"She'll have to see Tim," he said. "Next Tuesday at ten is the earliest she can work him in. He might open up a bit more to her than he has to us."

"Because she's a shrink?"

Nathan shook his head. "More because she looks like everyone's vision of the ideal grandmother."

Jade felt annoyed at her spurt of relief when he described Gert as grandmotherly. Why should she care? Tucking her legs up under her, she said, "I was surprised at a psychiatrist practicing in a small town like Tourmaline.''

"Shrinks are everywhere these days. Actually, Gert returned to her hometown when she retired from the Las Vegas group she was with. But she got bored and began taking on a few carefully selected patients. Now she has more than she wants.''

Jade nodded, shifting position for what seemed like the hundredth time, wondering if he could sense what was causing her restlessness. If she'd sat next to him on the couch the way she wanted to... But no, that way led to trouble.

If a relationship, no matter how hot the chemistry, didn't have a chance to amount to anything more than sex, she wanted no part of it. Sure, seeing him in those swim trunks had made her drool, but one-week stands had never been her style. In any case, Tim's presence in her house would keep her errant hormones from overriding her good sense.

Nathan glanced at his watch. "I'd better get going. I told the guy covering for me that I'd be back by ten.''

What was it now—eight? Since it wouldn't take him two hours to get home, she had to believe she was boring him. She'd been accused of other things by other men, but none had ever as much as insinuated she bored them.

Jade rose, hoping she was projecting a here's-your-hat-what's-your-hurry attitude. If he was ready to leave early, she was ready to be rid of him.

"I'll say goodbye to Tim and be off, then,'' he told her, getting to his feet.

Fortunately Tim was engrossed with the movie and let Nathan go without fuss. So did she, if you didn't count her hesitation at the front door when it seemed he might want to exchange a farewell kiss. Either she misjudged his intent or he changed his mind because no kiss materialized.

Losing your touch, are you, girl? she chided herself as she closed the door behind him.

The next day, armed with evidence a doctor had begun Tim's immunizations, Jade enrolled him in the private preschool in Carson City that her nephew and niece attended. She attended Monday's session with Tim, whose shyness evaporated as soon as he spotted Danny and Yasmin.

The following day he was eager to return and sulked when she told him he would be going to school only on Monday, Wednesday and Friday, like his new friends.

He got even gloomier when she told him they were going to see a lady doctor. Even when she said Dr. Severin just wanted to talk to him—no exam or shots—Tim still scowled. He finally lightened up when she promised to stop at Zed's ranch on the way back.

Dr. Severin, white-haired and casually dressed, didn't seem to frighten Tim. He wasn't happy about Jade's having to stay in the waiting room rather than accompanying him inside, but, clutching Freddie, he went without fuss.

Jade couldn't settle to so much as glancing at a magazine. Some mother she made, worrying about a psychiatrist frightening him, when she knew perfectly well Dr. Severin would do her educated best not to scare him.

When the doctor finally shepherded Tim back to her, all she told Jade was that she'd back up Nathan as far as police questioning Tim went. It definitely should not be done.

"I'll call you this evening between seven and eight, if that's convenient," Dr. Severin added.

Back in the truck, Jade couldn't resist asking Tim, "Did you think the doctor was okay?"

He nodded.

She held back anything else, aware she shouldn't probe and wasn't likely to get anything back if she did.

At Zed's, Tim went off with Danny, not giving her a backward glance, returning a few minutes later to say, "Danny says I can come here after school tomorrow, okay?"

Jade glanced at Karen.

"Fine with me," Karen said. "I meant to tell you that anytime you want to leave him here overnight, we'd love to have him." After Tim ran off again, she added, "When he's around, Danny and Yasmin don't seem to get into as many arguments. That alone makes him welcome."

Karen went on to discuss some new petroglyph findings out near Pyramid Lake. "I know you're interested in local Native American culture," she said. "They think these are even older than the ones near Fallon. The Paiutes at Pyramid say the Ancient Ones drew them, people who were there before them."

Jade made a mental note to check out the petroglyphs when she had a chance.

That evening, when Dr. Severin called at seven-thirty, Jade took the call in her bedroom for privacy, even though Tim was preoccupied with a new jigsaw puzzle.

"When I asked him why he didn't want to talk to me," the doctor said, "Tim told me he wasn't supposed to remember. I took that to mean he'd been punished in the past for mentioning anything about what he calls 'back there.' I'm afraid I got nothing else of any use except my observation that Tim is certainly a disturbed little boy, exactly as Nathan told me. Since he appears to trust you more than anyone else, my advice is to keep him with you as long as you can."

Jade hugged Tim a little longer and harder than usual when she put him to bed that night, aware their time together might end at any time. If only there was a way she could keep him forever.

Nathan called around ten.

"I spoke to Gert," he said. "We can stop worrying about the police. She called the sheriff and told him it could well cause irreparable damage to Tim if they tried to question him."

"She told me to keep him as long as I can," Jade said.

Nathan didn't reply for so long she wondered if he'd gotten a call on another line or something of the sort. "Tim needs you," he said finally. "But I think he needs me, too."

What was she supposed to make of that? That they share custody?

"I've been thinking that the two of us should try to do things with Tim," he went on. "Not just an occasional hot dog here after I give him a shot. We need to take him places. I've got a boat stored at Topaz Lake—maybe we could take him fishing."

Certain Tim would enjoy that, she started to suggest that maybe the two of them could go alone, guys together, but found herself saying, instead, "Set a day when you can take the time off and we'll be ready and waiting."

Two days later, Nathan called to say he'd arranged the fishing expedition for the following Tuesday afternoon. Jade agreed, forgetting until the next day that Tuesday was when Karen and Linnea were taking all the kids, including Tim, to the children's festival in Gardnerville.

She had an appointment to meet with a prospective customer that morning at his ranch near Tourmaline, but that wouldn't take long so she'd thought Tuesday was fine. Tim's excursion posed a problem, though, because he was eagerly looking forward to going to the festival.

She had no choice but to call Nathan and ask if he could set another date.

"I can and will," he said, "but since this is already arranged, why don't you and I go? We'll take Tim another time."

Go fishing alone with Nathan? Realizing she wanted to, Jade told herself there wasn't any danger in being with him in a boat on Topaz Lake, for heaven's sake. She liked to fish, and besides, it would give them a chance to discuss Tim without the boy being present.

When Karen heard about it, she offered to keep Tim at the ranch on Tuesday night and take him to school the next morning with Danny and Yasmin. "That way you won't have to pick Tim up and I won't worry about what time we have to get home from the festival."

Tim's instant enthusiasm when she asked him if he'd like to stay over at the ranch sold Jade. The closer it came to Tuesday, though, the more she wondered if she'd made a mistake both in agreeing to go fishing without Tim and also allowing him to spend the night at Zed and Karen's. Not that she worried he wouldn't be all right; it was herself she had doubts about.

Was she actually intending to spend a day with a man she was already far too attracted to, with the added problem of having no obligation to get home at any set time? A prescription for disaster if ever she saw one.

Chapter Six

Driving away from the Yerington ranch where the new well would go, Jade sang along with the tape—some real golden oldie about sitting on top of the world. That was exactly how she felt at the moment. The home well her crew would start on next week had come about because the rancher saw a Northern Nevada drilling rig up the road from him the previous month and went to see what kind of flow his neighbor got after they hit water.

Northern Nevada Drilling was its own best recommendation. It always gave her a lift to get a new job because of a previous drill where her well-trained crew had done exactly what they were supposed to do—hit water and get a good flow when they reached it.

If the day continued as good as it had begun, she

and Nathan wouldn't even have to throw out a line—the fish would be jumping into the boat. In case they didn't, she'd picked up some power bait with silver sparkles in the puttylike stuff you rubbed onto the hook.

Her grandfather had taught her to fish only because she put up a fuss if he didn't take her along with him and Zed. Grandpa couldn't help being old-fashioned in his ideas about what was appropriate for girls and what for boys, just as she couldn't help disagreeing with his beliefs, even though she loved him.

Because lining up the new well hadn't taken as much time as she'd allotted, she was going to arrive at the clinic before noon, not that it made any difference. Betty would probably just shunt her upstairs. She didn't mind waiting, not when it was her fault for being early.

She slowed the truck when she reached the curving potholed road along the river. When she came to the site of the accident, she saw county trucks repairing the blacktop. Or trying to. The road really needed to be completely resurfaced.

If it hadn't been for that accident, quite possibly she never would have met Nathan. At this moment she wouldn't be looking for the turnoff to the clinic. Or anticipating a glorious afternoon of fishing. Alone with Nathan, admittedly, but on such a perfect day she refused to think negatively. They'd have a good time fishing and that would be it.

As she'd expected, Betty told her to wait upstairs. In Nathan's living room, she turned on the stereo just to see what he'd been listening to. Country-and-

western, this time, a woman singing sadly about un-
requited love, which she found hard to relate to.
Maybe she was lucky that had never happened to her
because it did seem to be fairly universal.

Her problem to date had been trying to find someone she could love, requited or otherwise.

The phone rang, startling her. Four rings, then the
answering machine picked up, making her realize he
had a separate line for his private phone.

"This is Laura," a woman's voice said. "Just
wanted you to know I finally applied for another job.
It's a grant deal—I'll be studying wild horses. May
not get it but at least I'm trying. So stop worrying
about me."

Did Nathan worry about Laura? Apparently. Come
to think of it, he seemed reluctant to talk about her.
Jade wondered why, then shrugged. None of her
business. Every family had its secrets—hers had been
no exception.

When Nathan finally came upstairs, she was reading a magazine called *Medical Economics*. When she
heard his step on the stairs, she tried to convince
herself that her heart skipped a beat only because
he'd startled her. What other reason was there?

"Sorry I'm late," he said as he came in.

"No problem," she told him. "I've been listening
to all those tragic tales on your country-and-western
CDs. Each song seems to be a story, most with unhappy endings."

He grinned at her. "Keeps me reminded things
could be worse for me. Give me a minute or two and
I'll be ready to go."

He left the bedroom door ajar when he went in. Jade frowned. Bad enough that she could imagine him stripping down to...what—undershorts?—without the knowledge she could actually watch him if she didn't mind playing "I spy." Damn this chemistry thing, anyway.

It was almost as though he was coated with power bait and she was a hapless fish, unable to resist the lure.

That image made her laugh.

"What's so funny?" he called to her.

"Life," she told him.

When he emerged from the bedroom in jeans and T-shirt, she realized she hadn't heard him play back the answering tape. "You have a message from Laura on your machine," she told him.

He nodded, ducked back into the bedroom and replayed it. Listening critically this time, Jade thought Laura sounded defensive.

As he came out, she said, "Occasionally my brothers try to reorganize my life. They're never successful because I like my life as it is. I'm mentioning it just in case you might be trying to do the same with your sister."

He shrugged. "She's in a boring, dead-end job with mediocre benefits, working way under her education level. I've been encouraging her to aim for something she'd at least enjoy doing."

"Sounds as though she's been listening to you."

"I hope so."

"Brothers tend to be protective."

A strange expression flitted across his face, reminding her of the look Tim got when he was about to shut down, and she wondered what she'd said that would cause such a reaction.

"Ready?" Nathan asked.

"Ready as Freddie the Frog."

"How's old Freddie doing?"

"He's spending the night at the ranch with Tim," she said, regretting the words as soon as they left her lips. Although she hadn't meant any kind of an invitation, it probably sounded like one. "The fish are waiting, so let's go," she added hastily.

In the parking lot, he suggested they take his Jeep since it had a hitch for the boat trailer.

"Mine has one, too," she said. "I think it might be easier to back the boat in with my truck—on account of your snowplow attachment."

"Oh, yeah, that. I keep meaning to take it off. Okay, let's go in your truck. Otherwise we'll have to pay for two park stickers, instead of one."

Which wouldn't have been that big a deal. But she decided to let it pass without comment. The clinic wasn't that much out of the way between Topaz Lake and Incline Village.

"Want to grab a bite to eat first?" he asked.

"I'm miles ahead of you," she told him. "I brought along an ice chest and picnic basket. We can eat in the park at one of the picnic tables."

"Great idea."

"Have you heard how Alice is doing?" she asked as they drove toward the lake.

"Meant to tell you—she's progressed to having periods of consciousness but hasn't been able to tell them anything coherent yet. No more about her on TV?''

''Not that I've heard. And no one is bothering Tim, thanks to Dr. Severin. If only...'' She paused and sighed.

''You want to keep him, right?''

She nodded. ''But he might have relatives who care about him. If so, think how frantic they must be not knowing where or how he is.'' She sighed again. ''I can't make myself really believe that, though. The other day Danny asked him about the scars on his back. Tim didn't answer. In fact, he didn't talk for almost a half hour.''

''If I can prevent it, that boy's not going back to an abuser.'' Nathan spoke calmly but his tone was lined with steel.

At the lake, once they'd eaten, Nathan hitched her truck to the boat trailer. He was pleased, though not surprised, at Jade's expertise in guiding the boat down the ramp into the water. By now he knew if she said she could do something, she not only could, but did it well.

Once they were both in the boat, he started the motor on the first try and guided his fourteen-footer out into the lake, thinking he'd never before gone fishing with anyone half as attractive as Jade. There was nothing unusual about her jeans or Tahoe T-shirt. Or the billed cap she wore. But she made them look spectacular because they were on her. He smiled to himself as he watched her check her rod and reel. Always concentrating on the business at hand.

Even by the gazebo in the moonlight when she'd

put her heart into their kiss. Whoa, Walker, he warned himself. The June sun's hot enough. Don't get all steamed up. This expedition's to catch fish, nothing more.

Gloria hadn't ever gone fishing with him. Or done much else. He couldn't recall a single woman, except for his sister, that he'd ever taken fishing. Laura had always enjoyed the outdoors—he hoped she'd get the wild-horse job.

"Think we'll try the other side of the lake," he said.

"I've had good luck over there before," Jade told him. "I don't think we'll be pulling in any whoppers, though. From what I hear the trout are plentiful enough this year but small. Due to the flooding, they claim."

"All changes and misfortunes are because of the floods, or so they keep telling me."

"Be honest—when you came to live in Nevada's desert climate, did you expect a flood like the one we had this January?"

Nathan smiled. "Being from the Midwest, I'm well aware weather is never predictable. Some would say, like women."

"But not you?"

"Women are people. You know any person long enough and patterns emerge. You can't predict all the actions, but you can get a fair idea of how that person will behave most of the time."

Jade stared at him. "Are you claiming you pretty much know how I'm going to act?"

No way did he intend to open that can of worms.

"It was a general comment, not specific. Besides, I haven't known you very long."

"In general, though," she persisted. "What traits of mine have you identified?"

Careful, man, take it slow. "What you know how to do, which seems to be one hell of a lot, you do extremely well," he said.

"Come on, you're hedging."

What else did she expect? "You're confident. Basically friendly but you don't suffer fools gladly."

"I like that phrase about not suffering fools gladly."

"Thank my grandmother."

"What else?"

"Okay, you asked for it. Persistent to a fault." He grinned at her.

She smiled wryly. "At last, a fault. It can't be my only one."

"Let's turn this thing around. Have you formed any opinions about my character?"

"Hmm, let's see. You're a caring doctor. You like and understand children."

"Faults?"

"Well, there's that snowplow. Procrastination. Laid-back—though that's not really a fault."

Then why list it with them, lady? "I prefer to think of it as mellow," he said.

She shrugged. "You're perceptive and you're protective of those you perceive as helpless. Plus qualities. Now it's your turn again."

"Like I said—persistent. Let's see... Nurturing. Maybe a tad manipulative."

Jade frowned. "Me, manipulative? What on earth gave you such a wrongheaded notion?"

Hit a nerve, had he? Should have kept his mouth shut. "Look, let's drop this. We came here to fish, not to argue."

"One of your problems is you go out of your way to avoid confrontations," she accused. "You don't seem to realize that's a quick way to get differences into the open and discuss them."

"I have another definition of confrontations. In my experience they escalate problems, not solve them. Compromise is easier if the other guy isn't boiling over with fury."

"Compromise?" Jade's voice rose. "One way is usually either right or the best way to do a given task. The other is either wrong or a poorer way. How do you think I'd ever get a well dug properly if I allowed every roughneck I hired to talk me into compromising on how to drill?"

"There's more to life than drilling wells. Or practicing medicine. I understand the need to set standards in both professions. Still, as far as medicine goes, science has fought for years against recognizing any alternative methods of treating patients. Only now are we coming around to understand and admit some of them do work."

He cut the motor so they were crawling along. "We agreed to fish on this far side of the lake. No compromise, just straight agreement, right?"

Jade gave a reluctant nod and busied herself with plastering her hook with what he recognized as power bait. She noticed him watching her and paused. "Want some?" she asked.

A compromise, her way of dismissing their argument, even if she didn't recognize it. "Thanks. I haven't seen the kind with the silver stuff in it before." He slathered some on his hook, tossed his line over the side and almost immediately got a strike.

As he reeled the fish in, he heard Jade shout, "Got one!" After that they both pulled in trout so fast that everything else was forgotten. It didn't take long for them to reach their respective limits.

"I guess this really is my lucky day," Jade said. "Yours, too."

"I can't deny our luck, even though it shortens the length of time we can fish."

"Yeah. Catching is great but part of the mystique of fishing is in the doing."

They smiled at each other, for the moment in perfect harmony. At last, he thought, a woman who understands what fishing is all about.

"If the sites were closer to Topaz Lake," she said, "I'd suggest we go take a look at the petroglyphs. There are some out near Fallon, and I hear new ones have been found near Pyramid Lake."

"I know what they are from pictures," Nathan said, "but I've never seen one in the wild. I didn't know they were to be found in Nevada."

"Maybe another time." Jade couldn't believe her own words. Was she actually suggesting a second outing with Nathan? The trouble was, petroglyphs wouldn't be something that would interest Tim very much, so they'd be alone together again.

"We should plan to go somewhere with Tim," she added. "He was torn today between being with Danny and Yasmin or coming fishing with us."

"I see the peer group won out as it usually does with normal kids. It's a sign Tim is adjusting. Must be your positive nurturing."

"You already gave me credit for nurturing," she said. Neither of them, she'd noted, had mentioned words like attractive. Or sexy. Maybe he didn't think she was.

"I took this afternoon and evening off," Nathan said as he steered the boat toward the ramp. "Since I'm covered, I'm damned if I'm going back home early. You're the designated driver—what next?"

Jade blinked. She hadn't thought beyond the fishing. Deliberately. She had, though, believed they'd be on the lake until late afternoon, maybe into the evening. "I'll think about it while we clean the fish and pack them in ice," she said.

"Remaining open to suggestions?"

"Even to entertaining them." She pointed toward the lights of the casino at the top of the hill. "If you're hungry, the food's not bad there. Or we could drive somewhere else to eat. I know a couple of good places in Gardnerville."

"Ever been to Cowboy Joe's in Tourmaline?"

Jade shook her head.

"Want to try it?"

"Why not?"

From the name, she'd half expected to hear the usual country-and-western music in the restaurant. What they were served with their meal, instead, was cowboy poetry recited in a husky drawl by a grizzled elder who certainly looked as though he'd spent his life riding the range.

When they'd finished and were walking back to her truck, she said, "Good food. I'm not too sure about the poetry, but I enjoyed the poet's delivery. Is he local?"

"He's a rancher up Yerington way—does this as a hobby. Says it beats asittin' and arockin'. If medicine had the mythic qualities of the Wild West, I might be tempted to begin writing poetry about it."

"And reciting it in Boondoc Nate's?"

He chuckled, took her hand and swung their joined hands as they sauntered along the sidewalk.

The dusk was deepening, sliding quickly into night. Stars twinkled into visibility, but the moon hadn't yet risen. As usual, with the sun gone, the temperature was dropping, but it was still warm enough to be comfortable.

How right it seemed to be strolling on this June evening, holding hands with Nathan. She savored the moment, telling herself perhaps they could form a real friendship without it developing into a doomed love affair.

"Since you have to drive me home, anyway," Nathan said, "want to chance my coffee?"

Without taking time to think, she said, "I prefer tea at night," more or less accepting his offer.

"A wise choice. Some claim they can walk on top of my brew."

As she drove toward the clinic, Jade decided that, since she'd committed herself, to be polite she'd drink one cup of tea, make her excuses and leave. Simple enough. No problem at all. Just a friendly closure to a fun day.

Once upstairs, she followed Nathan into the kitchen, where he shoved his share of the frozen fish into the freezer, washed his hands and began peering into various cupboards.

"Aha! Knew I had a stash of teabags somewhere around." He turned and held out a small container. "Your choice, Ms. Adams."

As she lifted out a teabag, her hand brushed his and that damned chemistry, quiescent all day, sprang to life. Why now, when they'd held hands while walking without any potent electricity? So much for figuring they could just be friends.

He shouldn't have invited her here, Nathan told himself as he tried to deal with the jolt of desire firing along his synapses. The day had been great. Despite the special awareness he always had of Jade, he'd begun to believe he'd found a fishing buddy with no other complications to the relationship. Wrong.

"So," she said as they sat across from each other at the small kitchen table, "how long were you married?"

What the hell was she bringing that up for? "Three years too long." His tone held a warning not to continue.

"For both of you?"

He frowned. "I was the one who filed for divorce."

"You still sound bitter about it."

"No one enjoys admitting he made a mistake."

"She must have made one, too, if the marriage didn't work."

He blinked. He hadn't looked at the breakup from Gloria's point of view. If he'd misjudged her, she'd also misjudged him. He wasn't as easy to manipulate as she'd figured. Which reminded him of Jade's disparaging remark at the barbecue.

"Doormat," he muttered.

"For heaven's sake, I thought we'd buried that."

"Apparently not," he snapped.

Jade scowled at him and sprang up so suddenly she overturned her barely touched mug of tea. The hot liquid splashed across the table and into his lap. He rose, cursing.

"Oh, I'm sorry!" she cried. Grabbing a dish towel from the counter, she hurried toward him. "Are you hurt?"

He warded her off. "It's not a third-degree burn, if that's what you mean." It stung like the devil, but he doubted he had more than a mild first-degree burn, if that.

Reaching into the freezer, he grabbed a packet of frozen fish and pressed it against the painful area. Cold to a minor burn reduced, even reversed, inflammation. Not to mention eased the pain.

Jade snickered, finally breaking into laughter. "I'm sorry," she said between whoops, "but I can't help it."

Realizing how ridiculous he must look with a slab of frozen fish pressed to his groin, he began to chuckle.

Later, after he'd changed to sweatpants, he returned the fish to the freezer. Jade, having mopped up the spill with the towel, was rinsing it in the sink.

"Tea really stains," she explained, her gaze dropping below his waist.

"Not that I noticed," he told her.

She averted her eyes, reddening. "Are you…uh, okay?"

"Nothing fell off. That's one hell of a way to defuse a guy, though."

"I really didn't have that in mind." Belatedly realizing that could be taken two ways, she quickly added, "I'm usually not so clumsy."

"I've noticed. Hasty but not clumsy."

"Let's not get into totting up pluses and minuses again. Although you're right, I am hasty. My brothers tease me about it."

"That's a brother's prerogative."

She wished she could find a way to let him know she really regretted saying what she had about him to her sisters-in-law. Apologizing didn't come easy to her, though, and it might be worse if she made an issue of it by apologizing. Because how could she do it without telling him she was wrong about her evaluation of him?

She wasn't yet sure she'd made that much of a mistake, although she had to admit he wasn't quite like she'd thought. Worrying over it made her uncomfortable so she tossed it aside.

"I'd better take off," she said.

"Just because I've slipped into something more comfortable?" he teased. "I assure you I'm harmless—tonight at least."

"Next you'll remind me that's it's all my fault. Which I can't deny. It certainly was a good thing we caught all those trout today—you never know when frozen fish will come in handy."

"I'll keep that in mind next time you visit."

She smiled, wondering if there would be a next time. Against her better judgment, she found herself hoping so.

Chapter Seven

Two days later Jade still smiled every time she pictured Nathan with the frozen fish. *Defused* had been the operative word, certainly, because they'd said good-night once again without so much as a kiss. Which was the right way for them, wasn't it?

On the following Monday morning, she was surprised to find Tim hadn't gotten up first, which he had every day so far. She frowned when she saw Hot Shot lying in the hall near Tim's open door, instead of in the kitchen tinkling his bell.

"What's up, cat?" she asked.

Hot Shot rose, trotted into Tim's bedroom and leaped onto the boy's bed. Following him, Jade saw Tim was still sleeping. If she was to get him to school on time, he had to rouse him, so she reached to touch his shoulder and was taken aback by how warm he felt.

Her hand was on his forehead when he opened his eyes. "How do you feel?" she asked him.

He opened his mouth—and sneezed. She grabbed a tissue and handed it to him. As he wiped his nose, he sat up. Apparently satisfied that Tim was all right, Hot Shot jumped off the bed and streaked from the room. A moment later Jade heard his bell tinkle.

"Hot Shot wants to eat," Tim said hoarsely.

"How about you?" Jade asked.

"Yeah." Tim slid from the bed.

Telling herself all kids had minor illnesses and there was nothing to worry about, she shepherded him into the kitchen.

But when Tim started to drink his orange juice, he took a sip, then put his hand on his neck. "It feels funny in there when I swallow," he said.

"Your throat hurts?"

He nodded.

Substituting the handle of a spoon for the wooden blade doctors used, Jade held his tongue down and tried to peer at his throat with a flashlight. Red, from what she could tell. Her heart sank. Strep throat?

Last year Danny had it and was really sick until the antibiotic the pediatrician had given him began to work. She must get Tim to a doctor right away. The clinic wouldn't be open yet, but she had Nathan's private number. Grabbing the phone, she punched it in.

When he answered, lowering her voice so Tim

wouldn't hear, she said, "Tim's got strep throat. You need to see him."

"I'll see him, of course," Nathan said, "but how do you know he has strep throat? Is it going around in his school."

"Not that I know of, but his throat's red and he's got a fever."

"How high?"

"I didn't actually take it, but he feels hot."

"Any rash on his face or chest?"

"No. Can I bring him in right now?"

"You do that."

After she put the phone down, she hurried to get Tim dressed, telling him they were going to see Nathan, instead of his going to school.

"Why can't I go to school and then see Doc?" he asked.

"Because you're sick and the other kids in school might get the same bug you have."

"I don't have no bug," he said crossly.

"By bug I mean germ, bacteria, virus, whatever," she said. "The thing that's making you sick."

"I ain't sick," he insisted. "I wanna go to school."

"There's no use arguing. You need to be examined by Dr. Walker and that's where we're going."

"You're mean," he muttered.

Jade looked at him in amazement. Tim had never acted like this. It must be because he didn't feel good.

Hugging Freddie to him, he didn't speak to her all the way to Nathan's.

Clinic hours hadn't started yet, so Tim was the first patient to be seen. Nathan took his temperature with one of the quickie thermometers, looked into his ears and eyes with various instruments, then down his throat, before listening to his heart and lungs.

"Here's what I'm going to do," he told the boy. "First I want to see what kind of germs you might have in your throat, so I'm going to take a swab and rub it around inside there." He showed Tim the cotton-ended stick before inserting it.

"Okay, now we dab the swab across a blood-agar plate, like this. The blood agar is food for certain kinds of germs but not for others. We put the lid back on, keep it warm and see what happens. If nothing does, then we'll know you don't have that kind of germ."

Jade was as interested as Tim in the procedure.

"Now I need a few drops of your blood," Nathan told him. "I have to look at them under the microscope so I can learn how the white cells in your blood are fighting the germ."

"Fighting it?"

"Yeah, your body has the power to zap germs. Sometimes it needs help, sometimes it doesn't. Now, this is going to feel about like that shot I gave you— you remember that—only it's going to be in your finger."

"Ow!" Tim said, then sneezed.

"All done. Watch me draw the drops of blood up into these tiny little tubes."

Both Jade and Tim stared in fascination.

"You can get dressed," Nathan said as he left the room.

He returned after what seemed ages, but Jade knew couldn't have been more than ten minutes. In his hand he held what looked like a pen.

"Since you didn't check his temperature, I assume you don't have a thermometer," he said, handing the pen-shaped container to her. "Inside is the old-fashioned kind that goes under the tongue and has to stay there for at least three minutes."

"Thanks," she said. "I keep meaning to get one of those new ones."

"He has a low-grade fever—one hundred degrees. At this point he doesn't need any medication for it. A fever is one of the body's defenses against germs. Heat kills many of them. Don't give him anything to reduce his temperature unless it rises over 101."

Jade nodded. "Okay. I have some children's stuff Karen gave me in case Danny got sick when he was staying with me. What about the prescription?"

"What prescription?"

"Surely you're going to give him antibiotics."

"He doesn't need any antibiotic. His white-cell count is—"

"But what about strep throat? He can't overcome that all by himself. He'll need—"

"Will you listen?"

Jade plowed on. "I know very well that strep throat requires—"

"Shut up!"

Startled, Jade did.

"Let's reach an agreement here. I won't tell you

how to drill wells, and you won't tell me how to practice medicine.''

"But—"

"You want your mouth stuffed full of gauze? Listen to me, dammit. Tim's white-cell count is low to normal, not high. A bacterial infection produces a high count. The streptococcus organism is a bacteria. Therefore, Tim doesn't have a strep infection.

"As a precaution, I took a throat culture, which will let me know within twelve hours or less if I'm wrong. According to the white-cell count, I'm not wrong. The count indicates Tim has a virus infection, and most likely he'll develop typical upper respiratory symptoms in the next few hours. The sore throat will gradually disappear and the cold will run its course.

"Since antibiotics are useless in treating virus infections, he doesn't need any. I don't prescribe unnecessary medication for anyone.''

"Are you mad at Jade?" Tim asked him.

"Yes." Nathan's tone was curt.

"Are you mad at me, too?"

Nathan took a deep breath and let it out slowly. "No, cowboy, I'm not mad at you. You've had a cold before, haven't you?"

Tim nodded.

"That's what you've got now, so you're not going to be really sick. Colds are more of a nuisance than anything else.''

"If I'm not sick I wanna go to school. Can I?"

"You go three mornings a week, right? If you go before Friday or possibly next Monday, you'll bring your cold germs with you and some of the other kids will catch it from you. That's not fair, is it?''

Tim thought it over. ''Maybe not,'' he said finally.

''You'll let me know about what grows on the blood-agar plate?'' Jade asked, not ready to let Nathan have the last word.

''Only if I'm wrong.'' Nathan's tone had been a lot warmer for Tim than it was for her.

Upset as she was, she almost missed Tim's low-voiced murmur to Freddie. Nathan, she saw, had heard him and was listening intently to the other language Tim was using. When the boy noticed them watching him, he broke off abruptly.

''How come you talk to Freddie that way?'' Nathan asked.

Jade fully expected a shutdown, but instead Tim said, '''Cause he's a frog and he understands me.''

''Good reason. You got any idea why frogs understand those particular words?''

'''Cause frogs are from back there.'' Now Tim's face took on his shutdown expression.

Apparently Nathan recognized it because he changed the subject. ''Ever seen a camel race?'' he asked.

Tim shook his head.

''We'll go to Virginia City on Sunday and watch one, okay?''

''Can Danny and Yasmin come? Yasmin's already got a cold so she can't catch my germs.''

Great, Jade thought. Why couldn't he have mentioned Yasmin's cold earlier, before she'd gotten all worked up about a possible strep throat?

"Have to ask their parents," Nathan said.

"Jade can do that."

Nathan glanced at her and she gave him a grudging nod. From the way he worded his invitation to the camel races, she didn't think he'd meant to include her. Maybe he still didn't. Fine, let him cope with three kids all by himself.

When she called Karen, it turned out that Yasmin had a friend's all-girl birthday party to go to on Sunday. Danny, though, would love to join them.

"I don't think Nathan wants me along," Jade told her.

"What did you have the fight about?" Karen asked.

"We don't fight."

"Oh, that's right, doormats don't fight. They just let you walk all over them."

"Sarcasm doesn't become you."

Karen snickered.

"The truth is," Jade admitted, "I may have stepped out of line a tad and he called me on it."

"You do have a tendency to be outspoken."

"You're a diplomat. Zed would claim I learned to talk before I was two and haven't shut up since. He insists the first words I said to him were, 'Bad boy.'"

"I wouldn't doubt it—he can be. My advice is to make up with Nathan and enjoy Sunday in Virginia City."

After Jade put the phone down, she thought making up was easier said than done. At least for her. If she'd been going to say she was sorry, she should have done it right then. Apologizing had never come easy to her.

She had to call Nathan about Danny going. If she could get the words out without choking on them, she'd tell him she was sorry. Not because she wanted to see the camel races, but because she'd been wrong. Why was that so hard to admit?

On Friday, after clinic hours, Nathan went up to his apartment. In the bedroom, the red light on the answering machine was blinking. The first message was from a doctor at Washoe Med, notifying him that Alice, now awake and alert, either had total amnesia or was faking well. The police hadn't found her fingerprints on file anywhere, so they still didn't know her full name.

The second was from Jade, telling him Danny was going with him and Tim on Sunday. There was a pause, then she added in a rush, "I spoke out of turn on Monday. I'm sorry." End of message.

He stared at the machine. Jade apologizing?

Gloria had often said she was sorry in the sort of tone that belied the words. He was fairly sure Jade almost never said it, but if she did, she meant it.

He lifted the phone.

Having had dinner at the ranch, Jade and Tim didn't get home until after nine. Tim's cold, thank heaven, was markedly better. Once she had him settled in bed and read to, she checked her answering machine.

"On Sunday I'll pick Danny up on the way to

Incline Village to get you and Tim," Nathan's voice said. "I should get there by eleven. We'll stop for pizza on the way to Virginia City. By the way, Alice apparently has amnesia and they didn't get a match on fingerprints, so they still don't know who she is."

She decided not to wonder whether her phone call had something to do with his "you and Tim" or not. Nor was she going to worry about Alice's amnesia. Instead, she inserted a Chinese-language tape from the library into her portable stereo, put on the headset and began listening to the words, trying to decide if they sounded like anything Tim had said.

On Sunday the two boys kept the meeting between Jade and Nathan from being awkward. Once in Virginia City, they parked off the highway and found a good viewing spot at curbside since the race was down the main street of town. The prerace fake gunfight, complete with a fake arrest, kept the boys amused but worked against private conversation. Then the camels were paraded by on their way to the starting line. Neither boy had ever been this close to a camel before.

"Yasmin said they got lots of camels in Kholi," Danny reported. "I didn't believe her till Daddy T told me she was right."

"Camels are funny-looking with that big thing on their back," Tim put in.

"A hump," Jade said. "Some camels have two humps. We don't have lots of camels in the U.S., but a lot of years ago the army brought some into Nevada because of the desert here. It didn't work out—the camels scared the horses and wouldn't obey orders.''

"So are these descendants?" Nathan asked.

"No. A few camels escaped into the desert and bred, but they finally all died. But then people got interested in breeding camels in Nevada and, since there used to be camel races in old Virginia City, the custom was revived."

The race itself fascinated the boys. "They run a lot different than horses," Danny observed.

Jade had never been able to understand how the riders could stand that lurching gait. As usual, not all the camels were interested in running despite the urging of their riders. One stopped beside them and turned its big dark eyes on the boys. Tim reached for her hand and Danny edged closer to Nathan.

Curiosity satisfied, the camel ambled on.

"Maybe the camel was looking for Yasmin," Danny said.

Puzzled, Jade asked, "Why?"

"He might've come from Kholi like she did."

Jade decided to let it rest there.

Tim didn't. "You think the camel might've known her?"

"Not 'xactly. It's like the frogs in our pond. They never let me catch 'em. You said you can 'cause frogs come from back there where you used to live. That place with a funny name."

Jade held her breath, hoping Danny would go on. Obviously Tim had told him more than he had anyone else.

"Frogs don't stink like camels." Tim held his

nose. Danny followed suit, staggering around, pretending the smell was threatening to make him collapse.

Tim giggled and imitated him, neither watching the finish of the race.

"Time for ice cream," Nathan announced when they got too geared up.

As they were eating their cones, Danny said to Jade, "We could go swimming at your house, Tee. I brought my suit in case."

"Yeah, let's!" Tim urged.

"I don't suppose you brought yours just in case?" she asked Nathan.

"It's still somewhere in the Jeep from the last time," he said.

Like the snowplow, she thought but didn't say. Today she was determined to watch what came out of her mouth. "I guess that means the motion's carried. Swimming it is."

In Jade's pool the necessity to interact with the boys kept Nathan from saying anything personal to her. Unfortunately it didn't mute the effect her appearance in the two-piece suit had on him.

Finally, unable to resist touching her, he dived beneath her and pulled her under, holding her next to him for a beat before she thrashed free.

"Gotcha," he said when they rose to the surface.

"That's what you think, Boondoc," Jade countered. "You just wait."

Danny climbed out of the pool and turned on Jade's portable stereo unit. Nathan, listening to the incomprehensible words pouring from it, glanced at Jade and found her staring intently at Tim.

Tim, swimming to grab the ball Danny had abandoned, paid no attention to her or to the stereo. Danny switched it off, saying, "Yuck." Spotting Tim with the ball, he plunged back into the pool.

"Looks like I can cross Chinese off the list," she said in a low tone to Nathan. "Both Cantonese and Mandarin."

He remembered her telling him she was going to research various Asian languages in the hope of pinning down which one Tim knew. Sounded as though the kid had told Danny what country it was, though he wouldn't tell them. He'd bet Jade would be on the phone to Karen as soon as she had the chance, asking Danny's mother to try to get him to recall it.

Pushing off from the side, he began a lazy crawl toward the boys, planning to enter the ball toss. He'd taken a few strokes when something—had to be Jade—grabbed his feet and pulled him under. He jackknifed his body, reaching for her. When he caught hold, he wrapped his arms around her and, still entwined, they rose to the surface where they stared at each other. He saw the pulse at the base of her throat throbbing as fast as his own heart pounded.

"You're supposed to say 'gotcha,'" he murmured.

Extricating herself, she said, "That's only when you're sure who's got whom."

Later, after a stir-fry dinner with rice, a favorite of Tim's, the boys opted for watching a Disney movie on the family-room TV. Jade and Nathan carried their coffee into the living room. This time he waited until she chose a seat on the couch. Considering that as good as an invitation, he eased down beside her and put his coffee mug on a side table.

"So what did grow on the blood-agar plate?" she asked.

"Nothing pathogenic."

"I overreacted. Mouth off first, think later, that's me."

Another apology? The best he could come up with in return was, "I realize you worry about Tim."

She nodded. "I got to thinking I was all he had. Which was wrong. He has you to care about him, too."

Like a family. Strange how quickly this child from nowhere had become important to them both. "We'll make sure to keep him safe."

Jade set down her mug and turned toward him. "If only he'd open up more so we could find out who he is and where he came from."

"Even if he did, Tim might not be able to tell us all we need to know. He's only five."

Jade sighed. "So young to have had such bad things happen to him."

"No more. Never again."

She held out her hand and he clasped it, feeling the calluses. Small, a working woman's hand. Holding it warmed him. More than warmed him. Don't lose it, Walker, he warned himself.

"There, we've made a vow," she said, her gaze searching his. Her eyes were pure green, no brown in the irises. Rare. And beautiful.

A Kholi princess? She'd denied the title, claiming

she hadn't been raised in a royal family like Talal, but looking at her, he realized she bore herself like a princess.

Next you'll be quoting Omar Khayyám like Talal, he told himself wryly.

She hadn't pulled her hand away as he'd half expected. His gaze shifted to her parted lips. He knew what he wanted, and since she hadn't moved away from him, chances were she felt the same. Whether she did or not, he couldn't resist. He wanted, he needed...

Jade saw something in Nathan's blue eyes—sapphire?—that made her breath catch. The vow they'd made had to do with Tim, but the way he looked at her made her imagine another vow, this one including only the two of them. She could sense the desire pulsing between Nathan and her, definitely not one way, but coming from both, intermixing, mingling, intensifying.

"I think we'd better..." she began, her words trailing away when he shifted closer. She forgot what she'd meant to say when his hand left hers to draw her closer.

She lost track of time and space when his mouth found hers in the kiss she'd been waiting for ever since that first kiss by Zed's gazebo.

Chapter Eight

Nathan couldn't let Jade go, wouldn't let her go. Her response told him she'd needed the kiss as much as he had. To hell with worrying about where this might lead. She was in his arms, and that was all he cared about at the moment.

Her lips, soft and sweet, lured him on, canceling all his doubts, firing him with anticipation of what lay beyond the kiss. She felt so good in his arms. He couldn't remember any other woman feeling quite so right.

No other lips had ever been so enticing, so responsive. He'd waited a long time for this second kiss and was damned if he recalled why he'd delayed. He wouldn't make the same mistake again.

''He's kissing Tee. Come look, Tim. Doc's kissing

Tee.'' Danny's voice was like being drenched with a pail of cold water.

By the time they disentangled themselves, both boys and Hot Shot were standing in the archway, staring.

Recovering his wits, Nathan said, ''You're right, I was kissing Jade good-night. An old Illinois custom.'' Which wouldn't make any sense to the boys, but he was having a difficult time making sense, anyway.

''So now that I've kissed her,'' he went on, ''it's time for Danny and me to hit the road.''

''The movie's not over,'' Danny complained.

''You've seen that one at least three times before,'' Jade put in, ''so you know how it ends. Tomorrow's Monday. School.''

''For me, too,'' Tim said.

''Sure thing, cowboy. *Buenos noches.* That's Spanish for 'Good night.'''

''I could sleep here,'' Danny offered.

I wish *I* could, Nathan thought.

''Not tonight.''

Danny sighed, apparently knowing from experience Jade's *no* meant just that. Nathan couldn't help wondering if she'd have said no to him, too.

''Let's get on it stat,'' he told Danny.

''What's that mean?''

''Stat's doctor talk for 'Hurry up.'''

Once in the Jeep, Danny fell asleep before they'd driven a mile. He roused as Nathan carried him into the ranch house. When Zed took him, Danny gazed drowsily up at his father.

"You know what?" he murmured. "Doc kissed Tee good-night. For a long time."

Kids and their big mouths. "See you," Nathan said hastily and exited.

By Tuesday Jade knew Japanese was not the right language. Korean was ruled out by Thursday. On Friday she was jolted when the TV morning news flashed a picture of Alice sitting up in bed, the newscaster asking if anyone knew this woman. He went on to describe the accident again, saying a boy had been in the wrecked van. Jade caught her breath when she heard her name mentioned as the boy's temporary guardian. How on earth had the media dug that up?

Tim, who'd heard and seen it, too, stopped eating. She did her best to reassure him, but he remained silent, hugging Freddie to him as they left the house to drive to school. She hadn't put the truck in the garage last night, as she sometimes didn't. When they reached the drive, a man sprang from nowhere and snapped a picture of Tim before she knew what was happening.

"Get the hell off my property!" she cried, but he was already scooting away, having got what he came for.

Muttering, she boosted Tim into the truck and climbed in herself.

"I don't wanna be on TV like Alice," Tim said, fear threading through his words.

She couldn't lie to him. "I don't want it, either, but I'm afraid you will be."

"What if *he* comes?"

"You're in my charge. I won't let you go back to anyone you're afraid of. Do you want to tell me about him?"

He cast her an apprehensive glance and shook his head.

At the school, she made certain those in charge knew Tim was not to be picked up by anyone except her, her brothers or their wives.

Later that morning she left a message for Nathan to call her. She'd tried to put off thinking about him and how his kisses made her feel, and she wouldn't have called him if the media attention hadn't upset her. Or at least she liked to think she wouldn't have.

He called back after twelve. "Why don't you and Tim go stay with your brothers for a while?" he asked after she explained the problem.

"I would, except for Talal. He's supposed to be keeping a low profile at the moment. Some kind of trouble in Kholi—that's why he's living in Nevada for the time being. I can't risk drawing media attention to him."

"You two could stay with me. No one's likely to track you down here."

"No," she said hastily, even as her breath caught at the notion. "Thanks, but I couldn't possibly."

"If you're not here with me, I can't protect you."

"I'm not asking for protection," she said a tad testily. "I thought you might have some suggestions."

"If more media people show up, you could ready a short written statement to offer them and refuse to answer anything else they might ask. Or hire a security service to chase them off if they bother you.''

"If? Are you saying you think this might be a one-time thing now that they have a picture of Tim?''

"Depends on how newsworthy they figure Alice and Tim are. No one, including you and me, really knows anything about her and not much more about Tim. There's not much meat to the story.''

"It's really scared Tim. He's afraid that unspecified *he* is going to find him once his picture's on TV. The abuser must be who he means.''

"Too bad Hot Shot isn't a guard dog. I can't get away this weekend. I promised to take call for the guy who's been covering for me. Why don't you and Tim join me tomorrow afternoon? I'll unearth my badminton net and we'll teach him the finer points of the game.''

"That sounds like fun. Any objection if I bring Danny and Yasmin along?''

"None. I'll stock up on hot dogs.''

Even though the problem hadn't been solved, Jade set the phone down feeling cheered. She didn't need protection. She'd always been able to take care of herself. Not that Zed hadn't always been on hand if major trouble threatened. Now he and Talal together made a really formidable team. But Talal had his own problems at the moment—best not to get him involved in hers. And since he was staying at the ranch until his house near Genoa was built, that meant Zed couldn't be involved, either.

No, she didn't really need protection; she could handle the media if need be. She had herself to depend on; she didn't need a man to take care of her. Somehow, though, she felt safe with Nathan, low-key as he was. Feeling safe wasn't the same thing as being dependent on a man, not the same thing at all.

Linnea had offered to pick Tim up since she had to drive to Tahoe, anyway, on an errand. When she arrived with the three kids, Jade, back from the of-fice, was listening to a Vietnamese-language tape as she gave Hot Shot his weekly brushing.

The kids burst in ahead of Linnea, Tim in the lead. He stopped short, his eyes widening as if he expected to see someone besides her and the cat. When his gaze finally landed on the stereo unit, he blinked.

Jade switched the unit off, realizing she'd nailed it. Choosing her words carefully, she said, "I was trying to learn a few words in your other language so I could talk to Freddie, too."

Tim stared at her, speechless. She was conscious of Linnea leading the other two out of the room but kept focused on Tim. "It *is* Freddie's language, right?" she asked.

Tim's nod was reluctant.

She reached out and hugged him. "I'm glad you're living with me, Tim, you and Freddie. I don't know what I'd do without you."

After a moment he hugged her back, then wriggled free. "I wanna stay here forever and ever," he told her before darting off in search of Danny and Yas-min.

Aware Linnea would keep them busy, Jade picked up the phone and punched in the code for the number

Steve had given her. Instead of a recording, a real live person answered, a pleasant surprise.

"Robinson and Riggs," the woman said. Fortunately Steve had warned her this would be who she'd reach.

"I have a message for Steven Henderson," she said, as per instructions. "Please have him call Jade Adams."

"Thank you." A click and the line went dead.

By the time he called her back, Linnea, Yasmin and Danny had left. Tim was busy completing the project they'd started with Tinkertoys.

"Steve," she said, "I just discovered Tim speaks Vietnamese. Will that help?"

"Any information helps."

She went on to tell him about the TV newscast.

"I saw the woman's picture," he said.

"Some insensitive sneak took Tim's picture when we were leaving for school this morning. You'll probably see that next."

"Be careful," he warned. "We don't know who might have heard about the boy living with you. With his picture on TV, you can't be sure what might crawl out from under the rocks. I'll let you know if anything turns up at this end."

Jade didn't always turn on her alarm system, but as dusk slipped over the edge into darkness, she remembered Steve's warning and activated it, explaining once again to Tim how it worked.

"It's so *he* can't get in," Tim said, nodding.

"Actually, so no one can," she corrected him.

Apparently reassured by the activated alarm system, he fell asleep quickly. Jade, though, lay awake for a long time, wondering what Steve meant by things crawling out from under rocks. Nothing good, that was clear, but just how bad could it be?

When she did sleep, she jerked awake often, listening. For what, she wasn't sure.

Saturday morning she saw no one lurking about the house when she ventured out to pick up the Reno paper. She breathed a sigh of relief when she found no picture of Tim. Nor was he displayed on the TV morning news. Maybe she was anticipating trouble that would never materialize.

She drove away from the house before noon, a talkative Tim beside her, telling her about how the hamster at school escaped the cage the day before and how they looked and looked. "I didn't look too good," he admitted, "'cause I wouldn't like to be locked in a cage all the time like Munchie."

"Did anyone find him?"

"It's a girl hamster. Yeah, Munchie's back in the cage. Safe and sound, teacher says. It's okay to be safe, I guess."

She smiled at hearing him echo her thought from yesterday. Feeling safe was a positive emotion. Not that she didn't enjoy teetering on the edge sometimes. But not where Tim was concerned.

When she reached the ranch she discovered a minor problem had surfaced. Zed had arranged with another rancher who raised camels as a sideline to take the kids over there for an actual ride on a camel.

Naturally a novelty like that overrode any other activity.

"Tell you what," Zed said. "You go ahead and take the three of them to Nate's place. I'll come by around two-thirty and pick them up for the camel ride, then we'll keep Tim overnight."

"You're always keeping him overnight," she protested.

"I plan to get even. How about all of us descending on you for a pool party on Sunday?"

"Potluck," Karen put in. "You provide the drinks. Nathan's invited, of course."

Of course? Weren't her relatives taking too much for granted? "He's on call for another doctor all weekend."

"Too bad. We'll catch up with him another time."

Since the kids had left with the men to look at the ponies, Jade told Karen and Linnea about calling Steve and why.

"Vietnam? No wonder Danny couldn't remember the word Tim let slip," Karen said. "I suppose my big brother didn't bother to ask you to say hello for him."

"He seemed in a hurry."

"I think Steve's always in a hurry," Linnea put in. "He's restless even when he's at the ranch on vacation. Maybe he should take a few lessons from laid-back Nathan."

Were her sisters-in-law never going to let her forget her faux pas?

By the time Jade pulled into the clinic parking lot, it was just after twelve and all three kids were wired, anticipating the camel rides to come plus the promise of badminton with Nathan. Not that any of them knew how to play it.

Seeing several cars still in the lot, Jade led them through the gate into the backyard rather than going inside and trying to cope with their energy in the apartment. The net wasn't up yet, but Tim spotted the ball he'd found on his last visit here and she soon had a four-way guess-who-gets-the-ball-next game going. Yasmin, she was pleased to note, not only held her own with the two boys but looked to be ambidextrous.

Tim spotted Nathan first. "Here comes Doc!" he yelled, pointing toward the screened porch.

"Who's hungry?" Nathan called.

The chorus of me's was deafening.

He'd gotten the grill heated between patients, Jade discovered, so in no time at all the hot dogs were charred and shoved into buns.

"You realize we're corrupting these kids with fast food," Jade said between bites. "Hot dogs and pizzas are practically all we ever feed them."

"That's what aunts and friends are for—fun and fast food. But all's not lost—I bought chocolate milk, not sodas. Calcium and all that." He grinned at her.

After they ate, Nathan put up the badminton net, setting it low. He and Jade had barely begun teaching the children the game before his beeper sounded and he disappeared into the clinic to use the phone. By the time he returned, all three kids were waving their rackets like pros, even though they missed the bird most of the time.

"Solved the problem on the phone," he said. "Hope my luck holds."

It did until after Zed and Talal arrived to pick up the kids. Nathan and Jade had no sooner eased into porch chairs when the beeper sounded again. This time he made arrangements for the patient to come to the clinic to be seen.

"I'll be a while, so you might want to wait upstairs where it's cooler," he told her. "I have the air conditioner on in the apartment."

Since all the activity in the heat of the day had her perspiring, that sounded good to Jade. Of course, her pickup also had air-conditioning and she could simply get in it and drive home. On the other hand, that meant admitting she was afraid to stay.

Jade Adams afraid? Of what? Nathan? No way.

Herself then? Certainly not!

Once upstairs, she decided to take a quick shower, then grimaced as she started to put her sticky T-shirt back on—it was positively wet. Looking in the closet, she found a clean T-shirt of Nathan's, green with a wickedly grinning Garfield on the front, and slid it on.

Checking herself in the full-length mirror on the door, she smiled ruefully at the fit—more than a tad too big. She might be clean and dry, but she was decidedly not sexy. Which was just as well.

Nathan had bought a spread since she'd last looked in his bedroom, a soft blue one. An attractive color, though lighter than his eyes and lacking their brilliance. She sat on the edge of the bed to pull on her shoes and socks, changing her mind when she felt the dampness of her socks. Since she didn't care to borrow a pair of Nathan's, she'd go barefoot for now.

Driven by an impulse she didn't try to control, she shifted around to put her feet up, then stretched out on the king-size bed. She wondered which side he favored, left or right? Or was he a roll-all-over-the-bed sleeper? Since he kept the phone and a clock on the dresser, not on a nightstand, there was no way to tell.

The bed was at least as comfortable as hers, maybe even more so. Cool and comfortable, she imagined she was lying in his favorite spot, her head on the pillow where his had been, her body covering the place where his had rested. The idea made her tingle with what she recognized with dismay as desire.

Enough of that, she warned herself and fixed her gaze on the ceiling, noticing for the first time it wasn't really white but a very pale blue. Involuntarily she yawned, then sighed. How easy it would be to drift off. Not that she intended to....

Nathan hurried up the stairs, aware he'd spent a good deal of time with the "emergency" in the clinic, which hadn't really been one.

He didn't hear music as he reached the top, so Jade didn't have the stereo on. Was she reading? He opened the door, looked around and didn't see her. After passing through the living room, he glanced into the bedroom and paused, smiling.

Jade, wearing what looked to be his Garfield T-shirt, lay asleep on his bed. In the too-big shirt she looked like a little girl who needed protection, not a feisty grown woman who insisted she could stand on her own two feet, no matter what.

He stepped quietly into the room until he stood beside the bed. On second thought, she didn't look exactly like a little girl, not with the soft cotton of the shirt outlining the enticing curve of her breasts. It was so long it hid her shorts, leaving his imagination free to play with the idea she wore nothing but the shirt. Maybe she didn't.

Which led him into shucking his shirt, unhooking the beeper, kicking off his moccasins and easing down to face her. With great effort he refrained from touching her—not yet, not fair while she was sleeping—and waited for her to wake up and find him there.

He could use some rest—he'd been up half the night seeing patients. Not that he felt like sleeping with Jade lying so close to him. He blinked a couple times, trying to keep his eyes open....

Jade eased closer to the warmth next to her. She wasn't exactly cold, but the warmth felt good as she fitted her back against the curve it made. She sighed and was sinking deeper into sleep when she realized something was now lying across her between her waist and her hip.

Hot Shot? she thought drowsily. Without opening her eyes, she raised her hand to push the cat off and onto the bed beside her. When she touched skin, instead of fur, she awoke abruptly. An arm! At the same time the arm tightened around her, pulling her even closer against what she realized was a man. Nathan.

"Jade?" he murmured, sounding half-asleep. "I thought holding you was a dream. Maybe it is."

Heart pounding, little fires licking within her, she said, "Not a dream."

He shifted her so she faced him, his blue gaze holding her as much as his arms. "Gotcha," he whispered as his lips met hers.

It was the truth, the whole truth and nothing but the truth. No part of her wanted to be freed from his embrace. She answered the question in his kiss with fervor, showing him her eagerness to start down the road of no return with him. There was nothing to hold her back, so why shouldn't she accept what he offered, especially since she felt she'd die if he stopped kissing her?

Making love with Nathan was what she'd wanted all along, and to hell with whether it was smart to get this involved with him.

Nathan groaned when his hand slid under the T-shirt and felt the warm curve of her breast under his fingers. From the beginning he'd wanted to hold her like this and feel her respond to his touch. Warmly. Eagerly. Fire, not ice.

Needing more of her, all of her, he pulled the T-shirt over her head and off, desire burning in him as he gazed at her beautifully shaped breasts. His tongue licked one golden nipple, then he put his mouth to her other breast, her tiny moans thrilling him.

She tasted so good he wanted more. Her skin

smelled faintly floral, mixed with her own feminine scent, one that drove him up further. His dream of her wearing nothing under the T-shirt faded when he discovered she had shorts on and, under those, panties. Both came off and he tasted her all the way to her essence, feeling her trembling beneath him, shaky himself as need consumed him.

"Nathan," she gasped, "now, please now."

Her plea hammered through him urgently, scattering all thought, making him tear off the rest of his clothes. A few milligrams of sense remained, enough for him to grope for what he needed before he rose above her and plunged into her welcoming warmth.

And then there was nothing but Jade, nothing but the two of them united in passion.

Jade clung to him as they swayed in matching rhythm along the road she'd chosen to travel. No man had ever taken her so far, had driven her so crazy with need. This was a journey she'd never made before. Then all thoughts faded in a dazzling, blinding blaze of sensation. She heard a voice cry out—her own?

It took her a long time to come down, to return along the road to reality. Even when she became aware of where she was—in Nathan's bed—they seemed surrounded by a golden glow.

Sometime—not now, but when she could think clearly again—she'd have to ask herself if their lovemaking had set a dangerous precedent. At the moment, though, all that mattered was nestling close to Nathan.

Chapter Nine

Summoning all her willpower, Jade refused to spend the night with Nathan, even though the temptation was almost overwhelming. As she drove home in the dusk, stars began to appear in the darkening sky. Talal had named the constellations for her, but astronomy was not her thing. All she was sure of was Venus, a steady brightness among the twinkling stars.

Venus, goddess of love. Although it was called lovemaking, she didn't believe what had happened between her and Nathan had any connection to love. Wasn't it more a matter of hormones? Still, that didn't explain this achy sensation in her chest, as if she'd left part of herself behind with Nathan.

She'd sworn not to become involved with him in what could only be a dead-end relationship as far as she was concerned. Somehow she hadn't been able to stick to that vow. When she was around Nathan, she behaved as wildly as Hot Shot did when confronted with fresh catnip.

You knew exactly what would happen when you stretched out on his bed, she chided herself. Maybe you blocked it from your mind, but deep down, you knew.

Jade sighed. She couldn't trust herself. Unless she wanted to get even more entangled in a relationship she didn't think could lead anywhere, she had no choice but to begin avoiding him. As of right now.

But she'd miss him, miss his quirky sense of humor, his teasing grin, his gentle firmness with Tim and how she felt everything was all right when she was with him. Too bad there wasn't a way to separate the passion from the friendship so she could still have a part of him. Unfortunately she wanted both.

Her style was not to give in or retreat, but in this no-win situation, a strategic withdrawal was the only possible answer.

There's no one else like him, a voice inside protested.

"And damn lucky there isn't," she said aloud. "One Nathan Walker in this universe is more than enough."

She'd always felt the right man would come along someday, a man who, while not controlling her or even trying to, would be strong enough so she couldn't control him, either. Most of the men she'd dated—macho types, she admitted it—had eventually turned out to be control freaks that she'd shucked with no regrets.

Nathan was different. He might want to protect her, but that wasn't the same as being controlling. She grimaced, remembering how she'd described him to her relatives. As happened too often, she'd been a tad too hasty to judge. Nathan was no doormat. Far from it. But she wouldn't say he was forceful, either. He was, well, he was Nathan. A man she'd have to give up now or regret it later.

Nathan, sprawled on the couch, flicking from one TV channel to the next, halted abruptly when Tim's picture appeared on the screen. Cursing under his breath, he turned up the sound.

"...whose name is Tim," the newsperson was saying. "Like Alice, he seems to have no other name. If anyone has information concerning the boy or the woman, please call this number..."

Somehow they'd latched onto Tim's name. Nathan noted it was a California channel, not the local Nevada one, so the news was spreading. Jade needed to be told. Glancing at his watch, he saw that she couldn't have made it home yet.

The downstairs emergency buzzer rang, letting him know someone in need of his help was at the clinic door. He rose, slid his feet into his moccasins and activated the door speaker, saying, "Be right there."

Before heading down the stairs, he picked up the phone, got Jade's answering machine and left a message for her to call him.

How empty the house is without Tim, Jade told herself. Evidently Hot Shot thought so, too, because he made several trips into the boy's bedroom before finally curling up next to her on the couch. She put aside the well-drilling magazine she was attempting to read and stroked the cat.

"We're on our own tonight, old boy," she told him.

She'd checked her answering machine when she came in. Four calls, the last from Nathan. The other three could wait until Monday for a return call and Nathan might wait forever. She didn't want to hear his voice tonight, not while she was still vulnerable. Maybe she'd miraculously grow a protective shell in her sleep and be capable of dealing with whatever he had to say in the morning. Or maybe not.

Actually she didn't want to hear anyone's voice right now, which was why she was ignoring the TV. Hot Shot's purring was about the limit of what she could tolerate. She tried to focus on the magazine again and gave it up. A sad state of affairs when the man she was determined to give up occupied every last brain cell she possessed.

And what about her heart?

Jade scowled and flung down the magazine, startling Hot Shot. He sent her a reproachful glare, jumped down from the couch and padded into the hall.

Wishing she hadn't agreed to let Tim spend the night at the ranch, she rose from the couch and wandered into the kitchen. She could use the boy's company about now. Remembering how he liked choc-

olate-chip cookies made with oatmeal, she decided
to distract herself by baking some to surprise him. A
double batch, since everybody was coming to swim
tomorrow. Everyone except Nathan.

Stop it, she chided herself. Keep your mind on the
cookies.

Nathan spent a busy night seeing patients and was
pleasantly surprised when he awoke on Sunday
morning to discover it was already ten and there'd
been no emergency calls since three. No call from
Jade, either. Why?

Come to think of it, though, she could have decided to stop and spend the night at the ranch since
Tim was staying there. Quite likely she'd done just
that. In which case, she probably wasn't home yet.
He smiled, thinking about her in his bed. Whatever
he'd expected making love with her would be like,
it'd fallen way short of the mark. It'd been like nothing else. Like more.

More may or may not be a good idea, but he
wasn't going to worry about it, not when he couldn't
wait to hold her in his arms again. Just imagining
her softness pressed against him turned him on to an
unbelievable extent. Whether it was fishing, badminton or lovemaking, Jade put her whole heart and soul
into the action. If he could have persuaded her to
spend the night, they could be enjoying each other
at this very moment.

Jade wasn't the persuadable type, though. Far from
it. She wanted everything her way. His smile faded.
If she was any type, it was confrontational. Much as

he desired her, he couldn't see a lot of hope for any long-term relationship.

His beeper buzzed, sending him to the phone to see what the next emergency was. And so went Sunday. When he finally surfaced into a space of no calls, the sun was setting. He eased onto the couch and turned on the TV news.

No channel had any mention of Alice or Tim. Relieved, he decided it must have been a one-shot thing, as he'd hoped it would prove to be. Jade still hadn't called back, but it probably didn't matter now. The ball was in her court, and he'd leave it there until she picked it up.

He was zapping a frozen pizza in the microwave when the phone rang. Involuntarily his pulse leaped. No patients had access to his private line. It must be Jade. Instead, he heard his sister's voice.

"I have an interview in Reno next week for this new job," Laura told him. "I won't have a lot of time, but I'd like to rent a car and drive over to see you."

"Great. Let me know what day and I'll have someone cover for me."

They settled on her calling him from Reno and, as he put down the phone, he realized he wanted Laura to meet Jade. Never mind how long or short their relationship was going to be or how little time his sister might have in Nevada, he damn well was going to bring them together.

Getting family approval, Walker? he asked himself cynically. He remembered when he'd brought Gloria home to meet his parents. Laura, he'd seen right away, didn't like her. His father had been as taken in by Gloria as he'd been, but his mother, though she'd said nothing against Gloria, had acted wary.

"Perhaps you should get to know each other a bit better before you think about marriage," she'd said to him privately. "Say, a year."

A year had seemed like an eternity to him, and he hadn't listened. He should have. Were mothers always right? This summer his folks were traveling through New Zealand and Australia, having finally decided that Laura was doing fine on her own. Even if they'd been home, though, he had no urge to bring Jade to Illinois so they could look her over.

Why did he have this weird notion that Laura and Jade should meet? Certainly not to get his sister's approval, since he had no intention of ever marrying again. And if he did mean to marry, Jade wouldn't be his choice. At best, marriage meant compromise, and he doubted if she knew the meaning of the word.

Jade's Sunday was filled with family. She would have enjoyed the day even more if thoughts of Nathan hadn't kept intruding. Sitting at poolside with Karen and Linnea while the men amused the kids in the water, Jade pictured Nathan standing on the edge of the pool in those damn swim trunks and felt herself melt inside.

"Jade. Yoo-hoo, anybody home in there?" Belatedly she became aware of Karen waving a hand in front of her face.

"Sorry. Guess I'm a tad out of it. Haven't been sleeping too well."

"Too many good-night kisses from Nathan?" Linnea asked, smiling. "That'll do it."

"Danny reported all," Karen put in.

"I didn't bug you when you were going with Zed," Jade told Karen defensively.

Linnea giggled. "I heard you gave Zed plane tickets for Christmas one year so he could fly down to San Diego and seduce poor Karen."

"If I hadn't, who knows how long this stubborn pair would have taken to come together. Why, baby Erin might never have gotten made, much less born."

"Linnea and I like Nathan," Karen said. "The guys do, too."

Jade sighed. "So do I. But it wouldn't work."

Her two sisters-in-law glanced at each other and shook their heads.

"Don't be so eager to marry me off. I'm doing just fine as a single."

"Maybe so, but Tim will need a father," Linnea said.

"I'll think about that when the time comes. *If* it comes. I don't know what I'll do if I have to give Tim up. I'm beginning to realize I need him as much as he needs me."

"The waiting must be dreadful for you," Karen said. "But with Alice's picture on TV, she's sure to be recognized by someone and identified."

"Yes," Linnea said, "especially since—"

"Hey," Zed called, pulling himself from the water. "Where's the food? I'm only the outside cook. And in case you've forgotten, Prince Talal isn't handy at cooking in or out of the house. When we dine inside, somebody else has to dish it up.''

In the flurry of getting things ready to eat, Jade completely forgot that Linnea had been cut off before she finished whatever she'd been going to say.

Later, after they'd all left, leaving her alone with Tim, they sat on the couch together while he chattered on about the camel ride and the new kittens in Zed's barn. "I got to name one kitten," he said. "It's a girl, so I called her Kim."

"That's almost like Tim."

"Yeah. She was pretty, like the kitten."

Jade held her breath, hoping he'd go on, afraid any question might make him clam up.

"*He* told me she died and got buried in the ground. Alice said no, she went to heaven where there's angels. So he hit Alice."

Swallowing, Jade ventured a question. "Kim is dead?"

"I guess. Are there really angels? I never saw one."

"I don't think angels can be seen. Who was Kim?"

"I heard him tell Alice she was my mother." Tim edged closer and leaned against Jade. "I can't remember too good."

Jade put her arm around him, snuggling him to her. "Can you be my mother?" he asked, looking up at her, his body tense.

She blinked back tears, longing to tell him of course. But she couldn't lie to Tim. "I want to be because I love you very much," she said finally.

Satisfied, he relaxed against her. Hot Shot chose that moment to join them, butting his head against Tim like he did when he wanted to be petted. "Maybe Hot Shot loves me, too?" Tim asked.

"I'd say so. As much as a cat loves anybody. He sure missed you last night. And so did I. But I'm glad you had fun at the ranch."

"Linnea's gonna have a baby. If you had one, I could play with it."

"Babies need daddies," she said. To prevent any further discussion of daddies and babies, she added, "How about some chocolate milk before you go to bed?"

She succeeded in distracting Tim until after he'd had a bedtime snack, gotten into his pajamas, was read to and tucked into bed with Freddie beside him and Hot Shot curled up near his feet. Sitting on the side of the bed, Jade bent to kiss him good-night.

Tim kissed her back, then, looking up at her with his big brown eyes, said, "I bet if you asked Doc, he'd be the daddy. Then you could have a baby."

Gathering her wits, she said hastily, "We don't ask people to be daddies. They have to offer." It wasn't perfect, but it was the best she could come up with fast. She hoped it was enough to prevent Tim from mentioning any such thing to Nathan.

Because the fact was, she'd have to see Nathan again if Tim ever had to be taken to a doctor. He trusted Nathan. She couldn't be cruel enough to take him to a doctor he didn't know.

Feeling exhausted, she went to bed without watching the news and slept the whole night through.

The next morning, after she'd fed Hot Shot and he'd gone out in back through the cat door, she was pouring cereal into a bowl for Tim when the doorbell rang. Going to answer it barefoot, she looked through the window and saw an Asian couple on her doorstep. An apprehensive quiver shot through her.

"May I help you?" she asked through the speaker.

"We are Tim's parents," the man said in accented English. "We know he is with you."

Jade swallowed. "Tim told me his mother was dead."

"Ah, yes," the man said. "Very sad for Tim, for me." He gestured toward his companion, who smiled. "I marry this woman to be his mother."

Looking at them standing there so patiently and looking so harmless, Jade tried to find a reason for not letting them in. Was her reluctance only due to fear of losing Tim? "Wait, please," she said.

Returning to the kitchen, she saw that Tim had stopped eating, his expression fearful. "Is it *him?*" he whispered.

"I'm not sure," she told him. "So I'm going to bring you to a window where you can see the man and woman out there. I want you to tell me if you know who they are. Don't worry, the door is locked and the alarm system is still on."

Tim, clutching Freddie, followed her to the window, peered out and drew in his breath.

"Is that the man you're afraid of?" she asked.

Tim shook his head.

"Do you know who he is?"

Tim gave a reluctant nod.

"Is he your father?"

After a long pause, Tim said, "Maybe."

Jade, hearing the uncertainty in his voice, asked, "Is this the man you were living with before Alice took you in the van? The man who hit Alice?"

Tim shook his head.

"But you do know him?"

"Yeah."

If Tim could hardly remember his mother, was it so unusual that he wasn't certain the man was his father? Chances were he probably was. Yet she still didn't like the idea of letting them in her house.

"I'm sorry," she told the couple finally, "but since I'm responsible for Tim, I'll require proof of who you are before I open this door. And I must tell you the house has an alarm system." Why she said that, she wasn't sure, but it didn't hurt for them to know any attempt to break in would trigger the alarm. Not that she actually thought they might, she was just being cautious.

"Do you have some identification? ID?" she asked.

The woman said something in what Jade figured was Vietnamese and the man nodded. "Excuse, please, what ID you want?"

"Tim's birth certificate."

The woman said something again.

"I get," the man said. Both of them turned and walked down the steps, heading for a large brown van parked behind her truck. She waited, watching them. The man started the van and drove away. To get the birth certificate?

She waited until the van was out of sight, then turned to say something reassuring to Tim. He was no longer beside her. "Tim?" she called.

He didn't answer so she went to look for him. Poor kid, she hated to see him so frightened. When she found him hiding in the back of his closet, he had to be coaxed out.

"They've gone," she said. "I didn't let them in."

"She told him to go," Tim said.

He must have understood what the woman said in Vietnamese, Jade realized.

"She said, 'Pretend, find another way.'"

Fear gripped Jade. Pretend? What did they mean to do? "Did she say anything else?"

He shook his head. "Munchie's safe," he said. "Nothing can get her in that cage?" He made it a question.

It took Jade a moment to realize he was talking about the school hamster. "You're safe in this house," she assured him. "Safe with me."

He didn't look at her and pulled away from her touch.

Should she take him to school? In view of what had happened, Jade wasn't sure that would be a good idea. "Look," she said, "why don't I call the office to say I won't be in this morning, and instead of you going to school, the two of us can do something fun."

"I guess." Tim's voice was barely audible.

"Okay, I'll get some shoes on and then we'll decide what to do."

Jade ducked into her room, ran a brush through

her hair and slid her feet into sandals. "All ready," she called when she came out.

Tim didn't answer, nor was he in the hall where she'd left him.

Jade sighed. Hiding again? How could she convince him she'd keep him safe no matter what? "Tim," she called.

When he didn't respond, she began searching again. After she'd looked everywhere she could think of, she called his name again. "Please come out," she begged. "I can't find you and you're scaring me."

Tim didn't appear and a niggle of fear shivered along her spine. Where was he? Passing the alarm pad, she stopped and stared. Deactivated. But it had been on, she'd swear to that. And she hadn't shut it off. There was no one in the house but her and Tim. She'd taught him how to deactivate the system, but she couldn't believe he'd do it. Why would he?

The front door was still locked. So was the side door onto the terrace. Not so the back door—although it was closed, the lock had been released. No one but Tim could have done that! Why? Where could he have gone? She flung the door open, shouting his name over and over. Hurrying into her small, fenced backyard, she looked all around. No sign of him. The gate was still hooked.

Tamping down panic, she rushed back toward the house. From nowhere, Hot Shot appeared, dashing ahead of her through the door she'd left open. She grabbed the phone and punched in Nathan's private number, praying she wouldn't get his answering machine. She closed her eyes in relief when she heard his voice.

"Tim's disappeared!" she cried. "I can't find him."

"When?" he asked.

"Just now." Calming herself with effort, she told him about the couple claiming to be Tim's parents and how frightened he'd been. "It looks like he shut off the alarm system and left by the back door," she said. "But he's not in the yard." Her voice broke on the last few words.

"It'll take a little time to arrange for someone to cover for me, but I'll be there as soon as I can make it," he told her. "Chances are he hasn't gone far."

His words steadied her. "I'll go out and look around the neighborhood," she told him. "Maybe he got over the fence somehow and went up into the pines behind the house."

As soon as she set the phone down, she headed out, going through the back gate and around to climb the hill on the other side of the backyard fence. No houses had been built on the steep slope, so the pines grew thick, their dense shade discouraging underbrush. Their aromatic scent surrounded her as she scuffed through brown needles searching for any sign Tim might have climbed the hill ahead of her.

"Tim!" she called. "Answer me!"

From somewhere below a dog began to bark. Startled by her shouts or for some other reason? Jade paused. The only people near her with a dog were a ways down the road. Could Tim have disturbed the dog? But would he risk the road when he knew the people he was afraid of had a van?

He didn't know any of the neighbors, so she doubted he'd seek a place to hide in another yard. Anyway, none of them were really close by. She still couldn't understand what had led him to leave the safety of the house. Blind panic?

She was verging on that herself. Where could Tim have gone? He must be somewhere nearby.

After Jade had walked along the road in both directions, asking all the neighbors who were available if they'd seen Tim and gotten negative responses, she returned home. Should she call the police? As she was trying to decide whether or not to, Hot Shot twined persistently around her ankles.

"I already fed you," she said absently.

The cat stood on his hind legs, raising up to put his claws into her jeans. "Ow!" she protested. "That hurt. What's gotten into you?"

Hot Shot trotted toward the back door, pausing in front of his cat door to look back at her. She stared at him and he gave an impatient yowl. Was it possible…?

"Do you know where he is?" she cried.

In answer, Hot Shot slipped through the cat door. Jade ran to the back door, threw it open and hurried after the cat. Hot Shot scaled the fence separating her property from the next-door neighbor's to the left, who owned several acres. At least half a tree-filled acre separated her house from theirs. As the cat jumped off the fence to disappear on the other side, Jade noticed that the thick stem of the grapevine growing along the fence showed scuff marks, and some of the leaves had been torn from their stems.

She'd never gotten a single grape from the vine but kept it for sentimental reasons because her grandmother had planted it. Examining the woody stem closer, she saw it afforded an easy climb up and over the fence if the person climbing didn't weigh too much.

Jade grabbed the fence top and walked herself up the vine, vaulting over and down onto the other side, hoping the cat was still in sight. She spotted Hot Shot sitting at the base of a big sweet gum with spreading branches.

Before she reached the cat, he sprang up the trunk and vanished into the leafy green foliage. Standing underneath, she gazed up into the tree, noting the wood nailed to the trunk in a series of crude steps. Above her head, she saw an old tree house perched in a crotch. From an opening, Hot Shot looked down at her. Next to him she caught a glimpse of dark hair.

Weak with relief, she leaned against the trunk for a moment to take a deep breath and then let it out. "I know you're up there, Tim," she said, "and I want you to come down right now."

When he didn't immediately respond, she added, "That tree house isn't a good hiding place, you know. If I found you, someone else could."

She waited. Finally a small jean-clad leg emerged, then a sneakered foot feeling for the first rung of the steps. She held her breath while Tim climbed down the trunk, worrying about him falling. When he was safely on the ground, she knelt and hugged him.

"Thank heaven you're safe," she murmured.

He hugged her tightly, trembling. "I got scared," he whispered.

"So did I," she admitted. "But it's okay now."

Yet she knew it wasn't.

Chapter Ten

On the way back to the house, Tim told Jade he'd climbed the grapevine before to look over the fence. "That's how come I knew about the tree house, 'cause Hot Shot goes up there all the time."

"He knew where you were," she said. "He led me to the tree house. Thank heaven. I was so worried when you disappeared."

As soon as they were inside, Jade called Nathan to let him know she'd found Tim, but got his answering machine. Hoping he wasn't already on his way to her place, she left a message. He had a busy practice, it wasn't fair for her to disturb him unnecessarily. After all, she could have called Zed.

That possibility hadn't occurred to her until this moment. Instinctively she'd wanted Nathan's help, not her brother's.

"Are they gonna come back?" Tim asked as soon as she set down the phone.

"I don't know. But think about it—this house isn't like a hamster cage someone can pick up and walk away with. You're safe in here with me and no one can try to force their way inside without the alarm going off at the sheriff's substation. When that happens, the police come to see what's wrong."

"I wish Doc was here," Tim said wistfully.

So did she. So much so that she began to hope he was on his way, after all.

After trying in vain to interest Tim in games, books and a Disney movie, she finally gave up and let him do what he wanted, which was peer out the window. She did the same herself from time to time.

Finally she decided this kind of behavior would never do. She couldn't call the police because she had nothing concrete to complain about—the couple hadn't threatened her, after all. Except in her mind, and that didn't make it a police case.

"We can't stay cooped up here," she muttered to herself. "That's acting cowardly."

"Jade, come quick!" Tim cried. "I saw their van."

By the time she got to the window, no van—or any other vehicle—was in sight.

"They went that way." Tim pointed to the right.

The road Jade lived on came to a dead end three miles farther on, so if it really was the couple, they'd be back. Watching the house? Staking it out? Her apprehension grew.

An hour passed without any sign of the brown van.

Had Tim been mistaken in what he thought he saw? And where was Nathan? If he was coming, he'd surely have been here before now. If he'd gotten her second message that she'd found Tim, he wouldn't come at all—but, if so, why didn't he call?

Making up her mind she had to do something more than sit around feeling trapped, Jade sent Tim to collect his pajamas, toothbrush and clean underwear and socks. She hurried into her room and flung a few necessities into an overnight bag, adding Tim's belongings when he brought them to her.

After hastily putting extra dry food out for Hot Shot, she exited through the front door holding Tim's hand, all but running to her truck.

With him buckled in beside her, clutching Freddie, Jade roared out of her driveway toward the road that would take her down the mountain. Although she glanced often in her rearview mirror, no brown van trailed her.

By the time she reached Kingsbury Grade down into Carson Valley, Jade felt herself relaxing. True, the traffic was so heavy she couldn't be sure they weren't followed if the van stayed several cars back, but now that she'd taken action, she felt revived. Tim, too, had eased his grip on Freddie.

"Maybe I know her, too," he said.

Startled, Jade glanced at him. "Know who?"

"That lady."

"You mean the woman who was with the man in the brown van?"

He nodded. "Maybe she was back there."

"In Vietnam?"

"Yeah. Before *he* came."

"The man you lived with? The one who hit Alice?"

"Yeah. He took me away. I didn't wanna go."

"Took you away from Vietnam?"

Tim nodded again.

Evidently seeing the couple had jarred some of Tim's memories loose. Pushing her luck, Jade asked, "Does the man you call *he* have a name?"

"Grandpa."

His answer astonished and upset her. His grandfather was the abuser? "Is he Vietnamese—you know, like the man and woman who rang the doorbell?"

Tim shook his head. "Like Alice."

"Does he have another name?"

But Tim apparently had told her all he was willing to and didn't respond. Peering out the side window, he asked, "We going to the ranch?"

"No, to Nathan's. I think you'll be safer there." Which was true. The couple could easily learn she had a brother in Carson Valley, but it would be pretty difficult to trace her connection to Nathan.

Tim smiled and murmured something to Freddie. Looking at her, he said, "Freddie's happy we're going to Doc's."

So was she.

Interstate 395 remained busy as usual. When Jade turned off to head for Tourmaline, she checked to see if a brown van made the same turn, but her vision was obscured by the cement mixer that swung in behind her.

Shortly after this, the narrow, two-lane secondary road began to twist and turn, following the river, and the cement mixer hung a left, sending up dust from an unpaved road. Jade saw no van immediately behind it, but the road's many turns made it difficult to keep track. As usual, there were very few cars on this potholed route.

"Pretty soon we'll come to the turnoff to the clinic," she told Freddie. The words were no sooner out than a van roared up behind her. A brown van! They'd been followed, after all.

Using the lane reserved for oncoming traffic, the van pulled even with her truck and began trying to edge her toward the right, toward the boulders separating the road from the river. She had her choice of ramming against the van or allowing herself to be forced into the boulders.

Jade sped up, but the van kept even with her. If she pulled to the left, the impact might well bounce her back into the boulders. How she wished she was driving one of the big drilling-rig trucks, instead of the pickup.

Suddenly there was a flash of red on the road ahead—oncoming traffic. Jade yanked her foot off the accelerator, ramming on the brakes. As the van tried to pull ahead of her, the oncoming vehicle, making no attempt to edge off the road to avoid a collision, plowed into it. Literally.

Tim's cry of, "That's Doc's Jeep," was all but lost in the screech of metal meeting metal.

"Stay where you are," she warned Tim as she parked as close to the boulders as she could and jumped from the pickup, her heart pounding. Was Nathan hurt?

She reached the Jeep as he was climbing out and hugged him as hard as she could, tears of relief in her eyes. "They were trying to force me off the road," she gasped.

"I took care of that." He held her tightly for a moment, then let her go. "Tim okay?"

She nodded and he turned away to inspect the van passengers, cell phone in his hand. Now that she'd calmed down some, Jade could see that, thanks to the snowplow attachment, the Jeep had suffered practically no damage. The brown van, though, lying on the passenger side, was badly crushed, making her reluctant to look at its occupants.

Nathan spoke into the phone, put it away, then tried and failed to open the driver side of the van.

"Are they...alive?" Jade asked.

He didn't answer, continuing to struggle with the door. Finally it creaked open and he leaned inside. "Help's on the way," she heard him say to the occupants.

He hurried back to the Jeep, grabbed his bag and returned to the van. Aware she couldn't do anything to assist him there, she said, "I'll put out some flares," before going back to the pickup.

Once the flares were in place to warn any traffic of the accident, she climbed back into the pickup to reassure Tim.

"Nathan's taking care of the people in the van," she said. "We'll stay in the truck until the police come."

"Is the copter gonna come, too, like for Alice?" he asked.

Not until then had she realized they were only a few miles from where Alice had been injured in the crash of her stolen van.

"I think Nathan called for the helicopter."

"After it comes, can we still go to his place?"

Shaken as she was by the day's events, that sounded like a good idea to Jade and she nodded.

"Doc saved us," Tim added.

Later, after the deputies had asked their questions and been told what happened, and the copter had transported the injured couple—who would live, Nathan had told her—to Washoe Med, Jade drove behind him to the clinic.

Once upstairs in his apartment, he sat on the couch, pulled Tim onto his lap, then motioned for her to sit next to him. He put his arm around her shoulders.

"Okay, we all survived. Let's talk it through," he said. "As our favorite shrink would say, that's the best way to get it behind us."

"How come you were on that road?" Jade asked.

"I was coming to your place. Had a emergency right after you called. A toddler swallowed a bunch of baby aspirin and needed his stomach washed out. Then it took me forever to arrange for someone to cover for me."

"They wanted to wreck us," Tim said.

"I saw that. I recognized your pickup right away,

saw what the brown van was trying to do and did my best to stop it.''

"I told Jade you'd keep us safe."

"You bet I will." His arm tightened around Jade. "Your turn."

She repeated her story of the couple coming to the door up to the point where Tim disappeared. "He has to tell you about that," she said.

"Hot Shot showed me a good place to hide, so I climbed up in the tree house," Tim explained. "But then Jade found me and so it wasn't a real good place to go."

"Why did you think you had to hide?" Nathan asked.

"'Cause they wanted to take me away and I got scared. But then Jade said we'd come to your place and I knew you wouldn't let them."

"*I* wouldn't have let them take you," Jade said, upset that he'd think she might.

"There was two of them and only one of you," Tim pointed out. "You said there had to be a mama and a daddy."

"We were talking about babies."

"Yeah, but Yasmin's not a baby and she's got Linnea and Talal. Danny's got a mother and two daddies. If you're gonna be my mother, why can't I have a daddy? I only need one."

Silence followed his remarks.

Nathan was the first to speak. "I agree that one daddy should be plenty. But first we need to find out more about Alice and why she brought you here with her. Anything you can remember might help."

"But I don't ever wanna go back to him," Tim protested.

"You won't have to." The finality of Nathan's tone was a promise.

"I was asleep," Tim said slowly. "Alice screamed and woke me up and I hid under the bed like I always do when he gets mad and starts hitting her. I saw her run down the hall by the bedroom, but he caught her and hit her some more. Then she hit him on the head with something and he fell down.

"Alice knew I was under the bed. She made me get dressed and go with her. We walked and walked. Then she found the van and we drove."

"Did the man get up after Alice hit him?" Jade asked.

Tim shook his head. "That's how come we got away."

When it was clear Tim was finished with his story, Jade said, "The man he's afraid of claims to be Tim's grandfather. Apparently he traveled to Vietnam and brought Tim to America."

"She tried to stop him," Tim put in.

"Alice?" Nathan sounded confused.

"No, I think he means the woman in the brown van."

"Then there has to be some connection between her and the grandfather," Nathan said. "A step toward getting this puzzle solved. Did you live in Sacramento, cowboy?"

He nodded. "I didn't wanna tell you before 'cause I was scared you'd make me go back to him."

Jade glanced at Nathan. Was he wondering, like

she was, if Tim's grandfather had ever gotten up after that hit on the head? Maybe Steve could find out.

"That's enough of a therapy session for now," Nathan said. "Why don't we go out and buy some food for supper? We can eat lunch on the way."

"Lunch sounds good," Jade agreed. "But supper?"

"You and Tim are spending the night with me. In fact, I think you should stay here until the police solve this whole mess. The two in the van will be out of commission for a while, but we don't know who else might show up."

Jade stiffened, sliding away from Nathan and standing up. What had she said about him not being controlling?

Before she could open her mouth in protest, he rose and set Tim on his feet, saying, "Ready, cowboy?"

"Can we really stay?" Tim asked, looking from Nathan to her and back. "Nobody'll ever find us here."

"I don't think anyone's looking for us," Jade said firmly. "Not now. You heard Nathan say the people in the brown van aren't going to be bothering anybody for a while."

"But what about *him*? What if he comes after us?"

"I'm going to call Steve right now and tell him everything that's happened and what we've learned. I'm sure he'll do something about your grandfather." Have the police check to see if the man's still alive, for one thing, she thought. Was it possible Alice had killed him? That would explain why she'd fled and why she'd taken Tim with her—he'd been a witness.

Tim didn't seem particularly reassured by her call to Steve.

"Maybe we can stay for supper," she conceded.

"And tonight? Can we stay tonight?"

Although aware she was letting Tim manipulate her, she also knew he'd been thoroughly frightened and so she gave in. "Tonight," she agreed. "But we'll go home in the morning."

After Steve returned her call, promising to alert the Sacramento police, they left the apartment.

Later, after a joint effort in cooking supper, even Tim helping, they sat down to a meal of rice and stir-fry, with ice cream to follow.

Like a family, she thought unwillingly. Like the mama and daddy Tim wants. Still, she admitted to enjoying the fantasy; Nathan seemed to, as well. Why not? A family was the basis of life itself, two adults to nurture the child. But in this case it was no more than a temporary illusion.

She still had a bone to pick with Nathan, once Tim was asleep. Which brought up the problem of where they all would sleep.

"In my bed, of course," Nathan told her. "There's plenty of room for the three of us."

"Whoa, that's cool," Tim said.

"I can tell you've been going to school," Nathan observed, giving her a wry grin. "Enlarging your vocabulary, for sure."

"I get to sleep in the middle," Tim added.

Since Tim was so enthusiastic. Jade saw no reason

to disagree. With the boy as chaperon, there'd be no problem.

By seven-thirty, Tim was yawning. Once in his pajamas and read to, he settled down in the middle of the king-sized bed with Freddie. They left the door ajar. Speaking in a low tone so she wouldn't disturb him, Jade confronted Nathan. "Don't you ever try to control me again," she told him. "I make my own decisions."

He gave her a blank stare. "Control you? What the devil are you talking about?"

"Planning that we should stay here. I agreed to remain here tonight because Tim's had a bad scare, but you know as well as I do there's no danger. We'll be perfectly safe at home."

"I said I thought you should stay here, and I still do think so. In what way is that controlling? Besides, if you weren't planning on being here overnight, why did you bring pajamas and toothbrushes?"

"That was before the accident. Since they're now hospitalized, I'm no longer worrying about what the Vietnamese couple is up to. We're no longer in need of protection."

"I'm surprised you compromised your precious independence by asking me for help in the first place." Jade heard the tight control in his voice and realized he was furious with her.

Her own anger escalated, but before she could deliver a scathing reply, a loud buzzer sounded.

"Emergency," Nathan muttered, and headed for the door to downstairs.

Evidently his coverage ended with nightfall. Whatever awaited him in the clinic took a while to tend to, and in that time she had a chance to cool down. Maybe she'd been too hasty in calling him controlling—she was inclined to be a tad sensitive about control. Overprotective might have been a better choice of words.

He was truly concerned about Tim's welfare, besides. It could be he was trying to protect Tim rather than her, but she came with Tim in a package deal. Once again she'd spoken before thinking it through.

Apologize? She hated the very word, it always made her feel she was groveling. Perhaps she took after her grandfather, who never apologized for anything. Probably because he'd always believed he was right. Of course, he hadn't been, any more than she was always right.

Or maybe she had some characteristics of the Kholi father who'd died before she was born. Talal was the only Kholi she knew, and she was well aware he had to work at not being arrogant.

Yet Kholi genes were no excuse for her, raised in America by a no-nonsense grandmother who'd tried to curb her impulsiveness and make her the lady Grandfather expected her to be.

"Okay, like it or not, I'll apologize," she muttered as she heard Nathan climbing the stairs.

He forestalled her by speaking first. "I got a call while I was sewing up this guy's cut hand in the clinic. I have to go out and see a patient. Be back as soon as possible, but it may take me a while."

It did. Jade got drowsy, so she put on her sleep T-shirt and crawled in beside Tim. She woke when

Nathan returned and came to bed, becoming overly conscious of him lying just beyond Tim, close but untouchable. She hadn't realized the situation would make her feel so frustrated.

In this very same bed she and Nathan had come together, sharing a passion she hadn't realized she was capable of. She imagined his arms around her, his lips on hers, heating her very soul. She bit back a moan at the thought of his hands and his tongue caressing her…

How in heaven's name could she expect to relax when she shared the same bed with him?

Tired as he was, Nathan couldn't go to sleep, all too aware of Jade on the other side of his bed, barred from him by the small body of Tim.

Though a small residual remained, he'd gotten over being annoyed with her. It had always been difficult for him to hang on to anger for very long, a characteristic that Gloria had exploited.

He couldn't recall ever wanting Gloria with the febrile intensity of his need for Jade. Jade had gotten under his skin in a way no other woman ever had. He smiled to himself. You might say he'd become infected with her, and the only cure was to make love with her as often as possible.

Or, perhaps, that was only a palliative treatment. How frustrating that he couldn't reach out now and pull her into his arms, taste her lips, her breasts, feel her soft warmth against him as he—

Damn. Aroused as he'd managed to get himself, he'd never get to sleep. Tossing restlessly, he almost welcomed the sound of the beeper when it went off.

He leaped from the bed, grabbed the beeper from the dresser and clicked it off, then picked up the phone.

Nathan's beeper roused Tim. Jade put her hand on his back, rubbing it gently, and he fell back to sleep even before Nathan had hung up the phone. She heard the rustle of clothes as Nathan dressed, and realized he had to see another patient.

It had never before occurred to her what a doctor's life must be like. Because he had a rural practice in a relatively isolated area, Nathan might get called out more often than many physicians, but she realized that most doctors would have to take some calls at night.

One thing about well drilling, the emergencies were almost always during daylight hours. And, if you knew what you were doing, the emergencies were few and far between. Doctors, though, couldn't control emergencies, no matter how skilled they were.

As she listened to him go down the stairs, then heard the roar of the Jeep engine, it suddenly occurred to her that, since she couldn't sleep, anyway, there was a perfect way for her to apologize to him without the need for words.

Chapter Eleven

After Nathan left the apartment, Jade eased cautiously from the bed so she wouldn't wake Tim. Padding into the kitchen, she began to poke into the cupboards and the refrigerator. When she'd amassed all the ingredients she needed, she combined the mixture for bran muffins, filled the cups of a rather battered muffin tin and popped it into the oven.

While she was waiting for the muffins to bake, she unloaded the clean dishes from the dishwasher and slid the dirty ones in. Then she made coffee.

The timer dinged to let her know the muffins were done just as Nathan opened the door.

"Something smells good," he commented.

"Muffins and coffee. Be my guest."

He smiled. "How'd you know I like muffins?"

"A natural deduction, given the state of the muffin tin."

"I inherited it from my grandmother—she called it a gem pan. By whatever name, I love 'em. All kinds."

While she put some of the muffins on a plate, he kicked of his moccasins, poured himself a mug of coffee and sat down at the kitchen table.

"Paiute myth has it there's a trickster lurking about," she said as she lowered herself into the chair across from him. "He delights in confounding humans every chance he gets. Sometimes I can believe it's true—especially when he puts words in my mouth that don't get edited first by my brain."

Nathan's puzzlement changed to admiration mixed with a touch of exasperation as he realized what she meant. Trust Jade to find a way to apologize for what she'd accused him of earlier without actually coming right out and saying she was sorry. He took a bite of muffin and, savoring the taste, decided no matter what she'd said, all was forgiven.

After the next bite of muffin, he asked, "How do you know the trickster is a he?"

"The stories say so. Who am I to doubt another culture's myth?"

"How come you know so much about the Paiutes?"

He listened while she told him about the delinquent adolescent boy she'd big-sistered by teaching him how to work on a drilling rig. "He'd rejected his Paiute heritage, so we learned about it together," she finished. "I was thrilled when Steve located the father who'd thought his son was dead and father and son got together.''

"Steve seems to be good at finding out things."

"If anyone can help with Tim, he can."

"Didn't you mention once that Zed and Karen tried to match you up with Steve?" He knew damn well she'd told him that. Was that why he didn't enjoy hearing her praise the man?

"One unhappy, failed marriage convinced him women were to be avoided—except for brief flings. That's not my style and he knew it. A very astute man, Steve."

Even though he liked the guy well enough, he'd had quite enough of Steve Henderson. "Failed marriages do tend to make us men wary."

"Oh? Why would you assume all women are alike? You certainly don't think all men are the same, do you?"

Jade could leap with both feet into a argument faster than anyone he knew. "No two *people* are alike," he said tersely and picked up another muffin. "These are comparable to Grandma's gems," he said.

"I'll take that as a compliment. I also take it you don't care to talk about your divorce."

"Not particularly, no. Among other things, what it did was persuade me that one try at marriage was enough."

"I've never wanted to get married," she said. "Not that I have anything against it, but I've never found a man I cared to share the rest of my life with."

Jade would certainly not make what he'd call a comfortable life partner. "No man, ever?" he asked.

She shook her head.

He grinned at her. "All of us men are alike, is that it? Too controlling?"

He saw she was trying not to laugh. She failed. "Touché," she told him.

Sliding down in the chair until he rested on the end of his spine, he couldn't recall feeling so relaxed with anyone, not for a long time. Jade was like family. The word had struck him earlier when they, with Tim, were getting supper—family. But not blood relatives, not with this intense physical attraction he felt for her. Need simmered in him.

"Your grandmother would tell you sitting that way will ruin your posture," she said.

"You must be thinking of someone else's grandma. Mine was not a nitpicker."

Jade sighed. "My own, actually. She and Grandpa raised Zed and me. I loved them, but they were never quite satisfied they'd done their best with me. Zed, yes. Me, no."

"So you're still rebelling?"

She blinked, finally saying, "Maybe."

"You sound like Tim with that 'maybe.' Where did he get this mother and daddy idea, anyway?" He watched her blush, wondering why.

"I think it came from his finding out Linnea is going to have a baby," she said as her color receded. "Also, his grandfather told him his mother was dead and buried in the ground. No heart, that man, in addition to his other major deficiencies. Anyway, Tim

wanted to know if I'd be his mother. I told him I
wanted to be."

Had she blushed because Tim had picked him as
the daddy? No way could that be arranged, no matter
how fond he was of the poor kid.

After a silence Jade said, "Okay, I've decided we
can eliminate controlling where you're concerned.
But you are a tad overprotective."

He started to deny it and paused. Could be she had
a point. "Possibly," he said after a moment. "I suppose it comes from way back, from the time I didn't
protect my sister when I should have."

"Laura?"

"Yeah. It was a long time ago, when we were
kids. She'll be in Reno for a job interview soon, by
the way. I'd like you to meet her."

So much for having nothing more to do with Nathan, Jade told herself. Here she was sleeping in his
bed and next she'd be meeting his sister. But there
was no polite way to refuse. Anyway, she was curious about Laura.

"I'd enjoy that," she said after she finished the
last of her coffee. "I hope she'll get to meet Tim,
too."

Nathan hardly took in her words. He'd had about
as much as he could take of trying not to notice how
the soft cotton of Jade's sleep T-shirt molded to her
breasts with every movement she made.

"Speaking of Tim," he said, "much as I like him,
I damn well wish he was sleeping at your brother's
ranch right now."

He watched her nipples tighten as she understood

his meaning and felt an answering tightness in his groin. Pushing back his chair, he got to his feet. "Jade—"

"No," she said, rising. "No, we can't."

He ignored her words. Reaching her in two strides, he pulled her into his arms and kissed her. She fit against him in the way he remembered, soft and receptive, but not passive. Far from it. An activist, his Jade, in every way possible, including passion. She drove him wild.

Though the kitchen was too cramped for lovemaking, he didn't want to let her go long enough to move elsewhere. He deepened the kiss, needing to hold her closer and closer, until their bodies melded into one. Her fragrance was as stimulating as he recalled, and he couldn't get enough of her taste.

All the reasons they shouldn't be doing this fled Jade's mind the moment his lips met hers. Being in his arms was so wonderful, so right. What did she care if their relationship wouldn't last? At this moment her need for him was a driving force so strong she felt it in the very marrow of her bones.

She twined her arms around his neck, the softness of his hair under her fingers. Her lips parted, inviting him, and she tasted the tang of coffee, the sweetness of muffins and his own unforgettable flavor.

He'd brought the scent of desert sage in with him to mingle with his clean male smell. If only there were no clothes separating them so her skin could touch his. When she was with Nathan, nakedness held a well-nigh irresistible appeal.

She knew the two of them, bound tightly together,

were swaying in the close confines of the kitchen. She half expected them to fall to the floor, but it didn't matter; the place was immaterial when he held her like this.

He startled her by scooping her up and carrying her into the living room. Not the kitchen floor, after all, she thought dazedly. The couch, instead. It couldn't be the bed because...

A sliver of rationality pierced her cocoon of desire. "We can't," she said, hearing the betraying hoarseness of passion in her voice. "Tim might wake up."

He dropped her onto the couch with a thump. "Dammit, woman, what a time you picked to remember Tim."

"Well, I'm right." She sat up and rearranged her sleep T-shirt, then ran her fingers through her hair.

"Who's arguing? We both know the kid's had enough trauma in his life to risk confusing him about us."

Jade nodded. "I think it's best if I spend the rest of the night on the couch. I'm not on call—you are, so you need the bed more than I do."

She watched him frown, then accept her decision with a wry smile. "Might even manage to get some sleep with you out of reach."

"Tim and I will leave in the morning," she said. "Thanks for everything."

"Want to make a list of what 'everything' includes?"

Slanting a wicked glance at him, she murmured, "My grandmother taught me that a lady should never be too explicit. Good night, Nathan."

* * *

Jade awoke to daylight and Tim standing beside the couch. "Where's Doc?" he asked.

Sitting up, she looked around. "If he's not in the bedroom or the bathroom, he must have gone out on a call," she said. "Sometimes doctors have to get up in the night to see sick people."

"You weren't in the bed when I woke up," Tim accused.

"I decided to sleep out here." Jade stood and stretched, yawning.

After she showered and dressed, she fixed them both a bowl of cereal, then saw to it that Tim got ready. "Collect Freddie and we'll go," she told him.

"Freddie likes it here."

She knew that meant Tim didn't want to leave. "We'll be safe at home. The people in the brown van won't be coming around."

"They're in the hospital like Alice?"

She nodded. "And their van is wrecked, besides. So we're leaving. Nathan's a busy doctor. We can't keep bothering him, okay?"

With a big sigh, Tim picked up Freddie. "We left Hot Shot behind so maybe he needs us to come home." His expression clearly told her that if it had been up to him, the cat would have ridden here with them.

"We'll leave Nathan a note," she said. "You can sign it, too."

Having the chance to demonstrate his newfound ability to print his name cheered Tim up enough so that, once they were in the pickup and driving along, he began singing a song he'd learned in school.

Jade didn't feel up to singing, aware that the threat represented by the Vietnamese couple had been laid to rest only temporarily. More immediate was her failure to break off the relationship with Nathan. She sighed, understanding she really didn't want to.

Tim stopped singing. "Are you sad 'cause we can't stay at Doc's?" he asked.

"Something like that," she admitted.

On Thursday evening Nathan called Jade. "I'll be coming to Tahoe early tomorrow morning, if that's all right."

"Why...yes. No problem." He could tell by her voice she was taken aback.

"Actually there is a problem," he went on. "Alice's docs at Washoe Med want me to bring Tim over to Reno in the hope seeing him might jog her memory."

"You obviously refused!"

"Let me finish. I talked to Gert Severin, bringing her up to date on all we've learned about Tim's background. Her take on it is this—the request isn't unreasonable and their meeting might not only help Alice but might also resolve certain things for Tim, as well. Rather than deciding for Tim, she feels we should discuss the matter with him. Together."

"I don't think he should be burdened with even knowing about it."

"Gert tells me Tim is made of tougher stuff than either of us realize to have survived as well as he has. He needs to have a say in his life, she believes, instead of others making all the decisions for him, no matter how well-intentioned.''

"She may be a psychiatrist, but in this case, I don't agree.'' He could hear her rising anger.

He wasn't going to argue with Jade since he knew she wouldn't listen, anyway. "I'll be there before eight,'' he said. "See you then.'' He set the phone down before she had a chance to say anything more.

Why did she have to argue about every issue? The last woman he'd choose to be in a relationship with was a confrontational female like Jade. Yet he couldn't deny they had a roaring tiger of a relationship, one he didn't want to let go of. He shrugged off the possibility he might not be able to.

The next morning a patient rang his emergency buzzer at five. Nathan sewed up the jagged laceration on the man's arm, not believing for a moment the story he was told about how "the knife slipped, Doc, honest.'' Obviously, given the location of the wound, someone else had inflicted it. Luckily the injury, though nasty-looking, wasn't serious, and since the man insisted he'd accidentally cut himself, there was no need to notify the sheriff's office.

When he finished cleaning up afterward, his watch said six-fifteen. He climbed the stairs to the apartment to shower and shave, then notified his answering service that Dr. Kaylin would be taking his calls until two. Once in the Jeep, he headed for Tahoe. Early? Nathan smiled. Granted. But he'd told her he would be, after all.

Jade, barefoot, gorgeous and sexy in yellow shorts

and a crop top, greeted him coolly, which Tim's exuberant welcome more or less made up for. Hot Shot, Nathan noticed, remained neutral.

"I thought we were friends," he said.

"Well, of course we are!" Jade snapped.

"I was speaking to the cat," he said, aware he was provoking her.

"Hot Shot may be a tad more careful in choosing his friends than I am."

"Are you mad at Doc?" Tim asked her.

"No."

"You sound mad."

Hot Shot chose that moment to pad over and rub against Nathan's leg.

Jade threw up her hands and began to laugh. "You males sure stick together. I swear the next cat I get will be a female."

As if understanding every word, Hot Shot gave her one of those inscrutable feline looks and stalked off, tail high.

"Come on into the kitchen for coffee," Jade said. "Have you had breakfast?"

"Just orange juice," Nathan confessed.

"We're having oatmeal and cinnamon toast."

"She puts sugar in the cinnamon," Tim added. "It's awesome."

"Sounds like an offer I can't refuse."

As they ate, Jade said, "If you like you can drive with Tim and me when I take him to school. We can talk on the way back."

Warning him off the subject? What the hell did she think he'd driven here for? He waited until breakfast was over, then said, "Hey, cowboy, Jade and I need to talk to you, okay?" Ignoring her glare, he added, "You remember Dr. Severin?"

"Yeah. She said I could call her Grandma Gert, only I was scared to."

"She's a real smart lady, as well as a doctor. She thinks you're old enough to make up your own mind about certain things."

Tim eyed him uncertainly, giving Nathan a pang. The boy was only five, after all. He took a deep breath and went on.

"The doctors at the hospital where Alice is called me to ask if I'd bring you to see her. She still doesn't remember anything, so she might not even know you. What do you think? Do you want to go or not?"

"Do I have to?"

Nathan shook his head. "You can decide whether or not to visit Alice."

After several moments of silence, Tim slid off his stool and picked up his frog. "Freddie doesn't want to," he said.

Rightly interpreting Tim's words, Nathan said, "That's okay. We won't go to see her, then."

"Will you still ride to school with Jade and me?" Tim asked.

Nathan glanced at Jade and she nodded—rather reluctantly, he thought.

"Sure thing, cowboy," he said.

Tim reached to the counter and picked up an empty paper-towel center. "I'm bringing this for Munchie 'cause she tore up her old one. You can come in and see her—my teacher won't care."

"Munchie's the school hamster," Jade put in.

"Been a long time since I've seen a hamster," Nathan told Tim. "I've almost forgotten how they look."

"Sort of like a rat, only lots cuter. In Sacramento they got rat's nests in the palm trees. Sometimes they walk on the wires."

Tim was opening up more and more, sharing parts of his past. Because he trusted them, Nathan knew. Trusted them to keep him safe. As, dammit, they would.

"I don't like rats," Tim added. "*He* told Alice they were smarter'n her. She got mad. So then he hit her."

The more Tim revealed about his grandfather, the more determined Nathan grew about never giving up the boy to such an abusive man.

"Maybe Alice don't want to remember," Tim said, a surprisingly perceptive remark for a five-year-old. "Maybe she don't want to see me like I don't want to see her."

"You don't have to go and visit her," Jade assured him.

"Yeah, I know, 'cause Doc said so. Is it time to go to school yet?"

I hope he doesn't think I always speak the unvarnished truth, Nathan thought. That's some burden to lay on a man. "I'm ready when you are," he said to Tim with a glance at Jade.

Tim chattered all the way down the mountain, telling Nathan about his teacher and the other kids in his class. "But my best friend is Danny," he finished. "I like Yasmin, only she plays mostly with the girls."

"Female bonding," Jade said.

"Is that how they learn to gang up and giggle at the boys?" Nathan asked.

"Don't be snide. Boys snicker behind girls' backs and that's worse."

Nathan grinned. She was always ready with a one-upper.

He followed them into the school and dutifully admired Munchie, the hamster, and, more honestly, the curvaceous blonde who taught Tim. He noticed Jade's raised eyebrows with secret amusement.

They left Tim and, on the way out she muttered, "Pat's married to a biker."

"Pat?"

"You know who I mean."

He had all along but pretended otherwise. "Tim's teacher? Why should I care who she's married to?"

Jade shrugged. "No reason. Just thought I'd mention it."

"Wouldn't happen to have a dragon tattooed on his left biceps, would he?"

"I haven't a clue. Why?"

"Sewed up a biker's arm earlier this morning. Striking colors in the tattoo. Seemed like a nice enough guy, if a trifle careless."

Jade stared at him. He'd veered off again, taking control of the conversation. Probably just as well. She should have ignored the way he'd ogled Pat rather than making that oblique remark. After all, why should it matter to her if he looked at other women?

Once again in her pickup, headed up Kingsbury Grade in silence, he said, "Well? You said we could talk on the way back to your place."

She shot him an exasperated glance. "You know perfectly well I wanted to wait until Tim was at school before discussing whether he should go to see Alice. You paid absolutely no attention to my request."

"I'd call it more of an order than a request. I told you on the phone that Gert advised us to lay it in front of Tim, not make a decision for him. I drove up to Tahoe to do just that. So I did. It turned out okay—Tim wasn't unduly stressed."

Jade bit her lip to keep angry words from tumbling out. She had nothing to be annoyed with him about, not really. Much as she hated to admit it, Nathan had been right in taking Gert's advice.

"Gert pointed out we're in a partnership because of Tim," Nathan went on. "He looks to us as he would parents, and like it or not, we have to act as a unit where he's concerned to keep from confusing him."

"That's true," she said slowly, "but it would be lots easier to do if you weren't so infuriating."

"Infuriating? Me?" He shook his head. "What we have here is a classic case of transference."

"Are you implying *I'm* infuriating?"

"Not all the time. Want a doughnut? We're coming up on a place that sells them."

No one could throw her so completely off stride

as Nathan. "Their coffee is undrinkable," she told him, giving up on having a logical conversation. "Besides, I've got muffins at home we can have."

"Ah, you said the magic words. I was beginning to think you were on the verge of telling me never to darken your door again."

She grinned at him, unable to keep hold of her anger. "I was considering it, but then I figured Gert wouldn't approve."

"Do I get coffee with the muffins?"

"Why not? Even butter, if I dare use the word to a doctor."

"Got any jam?"

That was Nathan, always pushing her a tad farther.

Of course, one of those pushes had taken her to a place she'd never gotten to before, a place she never could have reached otherwise.

She shook her head. Coffee and muffins, with maybe a touch of jam, was all she was inviting him in for. Nothing more.

Chapter Twelve

When they were seated in Jade's kitchen attacking the muffins, Nathan said, "She wouldn't look nearly as good as you do in your white swimsuit."

Jade put down her coffee mug. She? Who on earth was he referring to? How could she be expected to follow the quantum leaps in his thinking? Was it Pat he meant? She decided it probably was.

"I expect she'd be falling out of it." Almost immediately she regretted her tart words. Not only did she like Pat, but she'd been decoyed into cattiness, something she tried hard to avoid. Still, it was no more than the truth.

Nathan laughed. "Too much of a good thing, you mean? You may be right. Besides, she doesn't have red hair." He took a final swallow of coffee and then wiped his mouth with the napkin. "Mine's still in the Jeep, but I need an invitation."

This time she locked on to what he meant. So that was why he'd mentioned her swimsuit. "You're not supposed to swim after you eat," she said.

"We can always rescue each other by throwing in those swim rings the kids use." He stood up and stretched. "I could use the exercise. I haven't had time to jog lately."

"Do you ever take your suit out of your Jeep?"

"Haven't lately. But I did get around to removing the snowplow attachment."

"So I noticed. One change at a time, is that it?"

"Take sorry—I've been there. I'll pick safe anyday."

Jade made a face. "Safe can be boring."

"So, okay, let's go wild and swim."

In her bedroom Jade eyed her mirror image quizzically after donning the white suit, touching her undeniably red hair as she recalled his words. She felt on edge, pleasurably so. Only Nathan could make her spin through one emotion after another in such rapid succession.

When she got to the pool, he was already doing laps. As she slid into the water to join him, it occurred to her this was the first time there'd been just the two of them in the pool.

For a time they swam side by side in silence, then, as if by unspoken agreement, both pulled themselves from the water to sit next to each other at the shallow end. Hot Shot, she saw, was watching from a safe distance with his usual incredulous expression reserved for those who got wet on purpose.

"He doesn't like men," she said.

"Except for me? Obviously a cat of unusual discrimination and intelligence."

"Vanity, thy name is Nathan." She pushed him and he fell into the water.

He grabbed her legs and pulled her in with him, his hands traveling up until he held her in his arms. Water swirled around her, waist-high, doing nothing to prevent her from feeling his arousal. Denying her immediate stab of desire, she broke free and swam away from him.

He pursued and cornered her in the deep end where, with both of them clinging to the side, he kissed her with such intensity it was impossible for her not to respond. The next thing she knew, he'd turned her onto her back and was towing her with him as though she was a drowning victim. Which, in a way, she was.

They fetched up in the shallow end where he scooped her up, carried her out of the water and stood her on her feet. Wrapping his arms around her so she fit into him, he kissed her again, deep and hot. She savored the sensation of his lips on hers, holding him close, the faint taste of chlorinated water seeming as sweet as nectar.

After long moments she pulled away slightly to murmur, "You know this is leading us nowhere."

"You sure?" His huskily whispered words tickled her ear. "I happen to have a destination in mind."

Heat seeped through her at the thought of where

he was taking them. That wasn't what she meant, not at all, but it certainly was what she wanted, to take that passionate journey with him. Never mind anything past that, not here, not now.

Nathan unhooked the bra of her suit, sliding it from her shoulders so the fullness of her breasts pressed against his bare chest. He cupped her bottom to bring her closer, aching for the final closeness but enjoying the anticipation, not wanting to miss any of the pleasures along the way.

He needed to touch and taste her everywhere, to caress her until neither of them could wait any longer. When he felt her hand slide under the waist of his trunks, he caught his breath.

"Too many clothes," she whispered against his lips.

Moments later they were twined together, both completely naked, skin to skin, the way it should be. How soft her skin was, smooth as silk and far more arousing. He bent his head to her breast, her moans of pleasure tickling along his nerves until he had to fight to control himself.

He lifted her feet from the tiled floor, holding her against him as he made his way to the exercise mat at this end of the pool enclosure. When they lay together on the mat, he kissed her hungrily, his hand sliding over the curve of her hip down between her thighs.

"Nathan." Her sigh was a plea as her fingers closed around his arousal.

"Wait," he murmured hoarsely.

She paid no attention, stroking him until he had

no choice but to rise over her and ease into her welcoming warmth.

Jade raised her hips to fit herself to him completely, caught in such passionate need that nothing existed except making love with Nathan. His name echoed in her mind as her body echoed every motion of his, responding to an irresistible force that drove her up, up and over into beyond.

As in a dream she heard his cry of completion and knew he'd traveled with her all the way. Held in his arms in the warm comfort of the aftermath, she smiled, nestling against him.

"You are one determined lady," he murmured. "When you decide the time is now, there's no stopping you."

"Did you want to stop me?"

"You know better. But earlier, what was all that 'leading nowhere' business about?"

She relished the feel of him next to her too much to let outside thoughts intrude. "We'll talk about it some other time. Not now."

He ran the tips of his fingers over her nipple, sending a frisson down her spine as the nipple peaked. Leaning over, he ran his tongue around the nipple, causing more trickles of excitement.

"Ever swim naked?" he murmured.

"Sometimes when I'm alone. It makes me feel wicked."

"Not in company?"

Jade shook her head. "I guess Grandma was successful in raising a prude, after all. Something she'd certainly be pleased to know."

Nathan caught her gaze. "Am I company?"

Looking into those blue, blue eyes so close to her own, unsure what she saw in them, her heart skipped a beat. Company? No. But what was he? Her lover, yes. And more. How much more?

Suddenly frightened by the direction her thoughts were taking, Jade sprang up from the mat, cried, "Last one in is a three-headed frog," and ran to the pool.

They managed to shallow dive into the water at the same moment, both racing for the deep end. When she got there, she turned to push off only to be caught in his arms, held firmly and kissed. With neither holding to the side, they sank together like two linked stones.

Coming up sputtering, Jade grabbed the side. Nathan surfaced a second later. "See what you do to me?" he complained.

"If you'd drowned, it would have been your own fault."

"And well worth it. Too bad I didn't turn into that three-headed frog—I'd get two extra chances to kiss you. Since I gather you're really a princess, who knows what I might have turned into then?"

Without considering her words, she said, "I'll take you just as you are."

The tenderness in his smile slipped into her heart. "There's no other woman in the world like you, Jade." His fingers traced the outline of her mouth. "No other lips like this. No other eyes quite so green, no face so beautiful. As for what's inside that red head of yours—absolutely unique."

Lips parted, she gazed at him, fascinated.

"The rest of you is beyond my ability to describe." As he spoke, his hand slid down to caress her breast. "Although I could try by utilizing the braille method..."

Jade, raising herself by putting an arm around his shoulders, cut off his words by kissing him. As his tongue met hers, heat gathered inside her. Soon she felt an urgent need to be closer, and so she let go of the side to pull him to her.

The next she knew they were sinking again. When they came up, sputtering and laughing, without words they levered themselves out of the pool and, arms around each other, retraced their steps to the mat.

Jade marveled at how, when they made love, it always seemed to be for the first time, although progressively more uninhibited. As they lay in each other's arms afterward, she wondered if she'd ever tire of lovemaking with Nathan. The thought was both exciting and scary.

Nathan, drowsy and sated, savored the feel of Jade next to him. He felt no need to turn away from her; on the contrary he wanted to hold her and cherish her. If he wasn't so content at the moment, that thought might trouble him but right now he didn't care about anything but being here with her in his arms.

Much later, after they'd showered and dressed, he took a reluctant leave of her to go back to his Tourmaline clinic and the pressure of his practice. Jade, he knew, would be following him down the mountain to pick up Tim from school. He waved to her as he pulled out of the driveway.

Somehow, it felt wrong to be leaving her. If they lived together, they'd share tonight, too, and all the other nights to come. But living together, presuming she'd agree, presented other problems. Her house was in Incline Village, at the top of the mountain. His practice was miles away in Tourmaline, and he had no more at present than an inadequate apartment—especially if they were able keep Tim.

He intended to fight for that right, but it did mean two bedrooms at the minimum. Living together also had dangers. Would she eventually expect marriage? No way was he going to do that again.

Nathan sighed. Best to leave things as they were, sort of an if-it-ain't-broke-why-fix-it situation. Knowing Jade's independent nature, he had a sneaking suspicion she'd never agree to their living together, anyway, so he might as well discard the notion as a pipe dream.

As she drove Tim home from school, Jade listened to his chatter with half an ear, troubled by her increasing attachment to Nathan. Why, for heaven's sake, tears had stung her eyes when he drove away from her house, as though he was leaving for good. How had she let herself slide into such a state?

"Can we go to Doc's tomorrow?" Tim asked, breaking into her self-absorption.

"Not tomorrow," she told him, realizing with dismay she wished they could. "But we'll see him soon because his sister Laura is coming to Reno and he wants us to meet her.''

Tim didn't respond for a while. "Maybe I don't want to see her," he said finally.

"Why on earth not?"

"'Cause I don't want to give Freddie back to her.''

So that was it—he was still worrying about losing his frog friend and confidant.

"Laura's a grown-up. She doesn't need Freddie now. Besides, she already gave him to Nathan."

Tim didn't look convinced. Poor kid, he'd had so few things in his life to count on. "I promise you Freddie is yours," she said firmly. "You won't ever have to give him to anyone."

To her relief, in a few minutes he was chattering again about the kids at school, apparently reassured.

She wished she had someone to reassure her that she wasn't making the mistake of her life by getting so attached to Nathan. Too attached. The word *love* lurked just around the corner, she feared.

She'd never been in love with a man, not really. Temporarily infatuated with maybe one or two, but never in love. How could it possibly come to that with Nathan?

How did he feel about her? Oh, he wanted her in the same way she wanted him, but she really didn't know if it went beyond that with him.

"To hell with love," she muttered.

"You said a word we don't use," Tim told her, sounding remarkably like his teacher, Pat.

"Sorry."

And sorry, too, she'd brought Pat to mind. Had she actually been jealous of the way Nathan looked at Pat? Obviously, otherwise she wouldn't have made the remark about the woman being married to a biker. A fine state she'd worked herself into. What had happened to the old Jade, the one who always kept in control?

"I know a lot of words we don't say," Tim went on.

"Me, too," she confessed. "But if you don't tell anyone, I won't, either."

Tim giggled. "Okay. You know what? Munchie's gonna get a husband so they can have babies. Hamsters have more'n one baby at a time."

Deciding to spike any future mention of adopting one of the pending hamster offspring, Jade said, "Hot Shot wouldn't like it if we brought home a baby hamster. He'd keep trying to get into the cage to catch the poor little thing. Cats think hamsters are like mice."

"Yeah, I guess. Anyway, Hot Shot was there first and he's my friend. Friends are 'portant." Again he sounded like his teacher.

Friends *were* important. If her relationship with Nathan blew up in her face, would their friendship be destroyed, as well? She feared so.

Shaking her head, she tried to put him out of her mind. He occupied far too much of her thoughts as it was.

Nathan called on Thursday evening. When she heard his voice on the phone, her heart pounded like that of a teenager hearing from the boy of her dreams. Although she'd refused to admit it outright, she'd been waiting impatiently for his call ever since they'd been together on Monday.

"Laura flew into Reno last night," he said. "She's got an interview tomorrow, but then she's free for the weekend. Think your brother would mind if I brought her along to the barbecue on Saturday?"

Damn that Zed! Here she'd deliberately not mentioned the family barbecue to Nathan so she wouldn't be tempted to invite him. Then what had her brother done? Gone ahead and extended an invitation behind her back. Not that she minded Nathan's being there at the ranch but what she didn't want was for her brothers and their wives to assume she and Nathan were a couple. Apparently they already did, though.

Well, done was done. "I'm sure they'll welcome Laura," she told Nathan. "I'll mention to Karen that she'll be coming."

"Thanks. See you then."

As she set down the phone, Jade tried to dismiss her disappointment at his terseness. What had she expected—some kind of heartfelt declaration of his intentions? How ridiculous! Still, he could have said a few more words. That he missed her, for example. Or at least that he was looking forward to seeing her on Saturday.

Maybe what had happened on Monday meant more to her than to Nathan. And why in heaven's name had it meant so much to her?

When she and Tim arrived at the ranch on Saturday, he left Freddie in the truck before running off to find Danny and Jasmine. More slowly, Jade carried her big bowl of coleslaw through the back door. She found Linnea sitting at the kitchen table rolling plastic cutlery into paper napkins while she watched Erin in the highchair.

"Tell me," Linnea said after greeting her, "did Danny go through a stage of tossing everything on the floor and waiting for someone to pick it up?"

Jade nodded. "I remember only too well."

"I missed that period with Yasmin." Linnea's tone was wistful.

Erin held out her arms. "Tee," she demanded. "Up."

Jade wiped the baby's face and hands, extricated her from the high chair and hugged her.

"Down," Erin insisted.

"The playpen's on the back patio," Linnea said. "We could sit out there."

After Erin was deposited in the playpen, Jade eased into a lounge chair next to Linnea.

"I understand Nathan's bringing his sister," Linnea said.

"Yes, Laura's in Reno for an interview."

"But you've never met her?"

Jade shook her head. "I hope all of us together don't overwhelm her."

"It's just as well she's able to meet us before..." Apparently Jade's stony stare changed her mind about what she was about to say because she wound up with, "I guess I'm speaking out of turn. Sorry.

Maybe we're paying too much attention to what Tim says.''

For some reason it hadn't occurred to Jade that Tim might be telling Danny and Yasmin everything he and Jade did. She flushed, realizing how the fact that she and Tim had spent the night at Nathan's could be interpreted.

At that moment Karen appeared around the corner of the house. She plopped down in a chair on the other side of Linnea and said, ''What's new?''

''I am definitely not engaged to Nathan, if that's what you mean,'' Jade said tartly. ''Nor do I anticipate such a thing ever happening.''

''It sounds as though you two had a spat.''

Jade rolled her eyes. ''There is such a thing as a man and a woman just being friends.''

Karen gave her a knowing look. ''Of course.''

Deliberately turning to Linnea, Jade asked, ''How's the house coming?''

They were discussing the vagaries of contractors when Tim ran onto the patio and grabbed her hand, urging her up. ''Doc's here. We gotta go meet him.''

Deciding the courteous thing to do was to meet Laura first so she could try to introduce her gradually to the others, she followed Tim toward the parking area. But her gaze went first to Nathan, looking like a true Nevadan in faded jeans and a Tourmaline T-shirt. A damned handsome Nevadan.

His sister stood partly behind him as though using him for a shield against the unknown. Laura was prettier than she'd looked in the photo, although pale. She wore her long blond hair in a French braid and

her eyes were not as blue as Nathan's—more gray-
ish.

Tim, gripping Nathan's hand, stared apprehensively at her. "You're Laura," he said before Jade
could greet her.

Laura smiled at him. "And you're Tim."

"Doc gave me Freddie," Tim said. "He's mine
now."

Laura blinked, obviously not tracking.

"He means Frederick Ferdinand Frog," Nathan
explained. "Tim has an affinity for frogs and Freddie's become his friend."

"Tim knows Freddie was once yours," Jade told
Laura. "He's been worried you might want him
back."

At Nathan's mention of the frog, Laura's face had
gone blank. Now she shook her head slightly and
crouched beside Tim, coming down to his level.

"I needed Freddie once, but I don't anymore," she
said. "I know Freddie wants to be with someone who
needs him—like you. He's yours for as long as you
decide to keep him."

Tim offered her a tentative smile, then gestured
toward the pickup. "He's in there if you want to say
hello."

"Thank you, Tim, that's very generous of you,"
Laura said. "But Freddie and I don't have anything
to talk about anymore. You can say hello for me
later."

"Okay. He'll remember you 'cause he doesn't forget anything." Danny shouted Tim's name and he
ran off, calling, "See you," over his shoulder.

Jade held out her hand to Laura. "As you may have gathered during this rather unorthodox meeting, I'm Jade Adams."

Laura shook her hand. "Tim's a sweetheart. I can see why Nathan's so fond of him. Obviously you are, too."

They began to walk toward the house but were intercepted by Zed and Talal before reaching it. Laura's reaction was to hang back, so once again she stood slightly behind Nathan. Jade's curiosity was aroused. Laura hadn't seemed particularly shy, but maybe she was.

Jade watched while her brothers, as usual in the presence of a pretty woman, tried their best to charm her socks off.

Laura's response was polite but guarded; she was nowhere near as free and easy as she'd been with Tim. Zed and Talal bore Nathan off, leaving Jade to bring Laura to meet the others.

With the women, Laura seemed to relax, telling them they'd snagged the two most attractive men she'd ever seen. "In duplicate, yet. Unbelievable," she added.

Just shy with men, maybe, Jade decided.

"Do show Laura around," Karen urged. "Linnea and I will have cold drinks fixed when you get back."

When they reached the gazebo by the pond, Laura climbed the steps and sat down inside, saying, "How charming." She gazed toward the mountains, their peaks now bare of snow due to the hot summer sun. "I had no idea Nevada was so beautiful."

"People from other states are always surprised," Jade said, joining her.

"Nathan told me you've always lived here." She glanced appraisingly at Jade. "You're very different from Gloria, for which I'm thankful. She was a real bitch."

Gloria, Jade recalled, was Nathan's ex-wife. "He never talks about her."

"She tried her best to ruin his life. We were happy when he finally divorced her. I'm afraid, though…" Laura paused. "You won't be offended?"

"I doubt it. Go ahead."

"Well, it's just that Gloria so soured him on women that I don't think he'll ever marry again. I like you and can see why he's so fond of you, but…" Again she paused.

"But he's not apt to marry me, is that it?" Jade's words were lighter than her heart.

"I'm so glad you understand. I dreaded annoying or upsetting you, but once I met you I knew I had to tell you."

"I'm not too keen on getting married myself." As soon as she spoke, Jade knew the words, once true enough, no longer were.

"That's good. Nathan is a wonderful brother. He needs someone who won't…well, expect too much." Laura's smile was sad. "He and I are alike in at least one way—I'll never marry, either."

Jade's curiosity overcame her politeness. She was choosing the words to ask why when the three kids appeared, racing around the pond, Tim in the lead, pointing at the gazebo. The two women clearly heard his "There they are!"

"I suspect we're about to be invaded," she told Laura, instead.

Laura answered Danny's barrage of questions with patient humor and told Yasmin that, no, she'd never ridden on a camel, but did know how to ride a horse.

At last Tim said, "We're supposed to tell you the lemonade is ready."

With the children scurrying ahead of them, Jade and Laura walked back to the patio.

With everyone together, the conversation turned general. Then it was time to eat. Later, Jade retrieved her guitar from the pickup and everyone sang folk songs. All three of the kids, she was amused to see, had learned a plaintive Kholi tune of Talal's.

Not once was she alone with Nathan, for which she was grateful. Exactly as she'd known from the beginning, any relationship with him could go no-where.

As the evening began to wind down, she offered to put a sleepy Erin to bed. As she was coming out of the baby's bedroom, she found Nathan waiting in the hall. Without a word he took her hand, leading her along the hall to the addition and out into the rose garden.

The perfume of the roses wrapped around her, and the moon cast its bewitching glimmer as Nathan paused and turned her toward him. He must remember, as she did, this was the romantic spot where they'd exchanged their first kiss. Bemused by that recollection, the rose scent, the moonlight and his nearness, she tilted her face up to him, eyes closing as she anticipated what would happen.

"We're getting in too deep," he told her, instead of kissing her. "I know neither of us want that. It's time to pull back and take a good look at what's happening."

She felt as though he'd slapped her. Tears stinging her eyes, she turned from him. With great effort she steadied her voice enough to say coolly, "I've been thinking the same thing. Now that it's out in the open, we can just go our separate ways with no regrets." She headed blindly for the door leading into the house.

"Wait," he said. "That's not exactly what I meant—too drastic. I—"

"It's exactly what *I* mean," she snapped, anger rescuing her from breaking down completely. She opened the door, pausing to offer a final, "Goodbye, Nathan."

Chapter Thirteen

As the days passed after what Jade had meant as her final goodbye to Nathan, she worked past her hurt enough to realize that didn't mean she'd never see him again. Any permanent farewell would have to be just for social occasions or anything one-on-one. Naturally Nathan was still Tim's doctor, and there also might be times he'd want to take the boy on some excursion.

More or less like joint custody, she decided, even though they'd never been married. Just separated.

A phone call from Steve modified her plans.

"I'll be in Nevada next week," he told her, "but I have a hunch the Sacramento cops will be calling on you before I can get there."

"What on earth for?" she demanded.

"Monty Martin's dead. My agency sicced them

onto Martin, and they found he was already on their books as a homicide victim.''

"Who *is* Monty Martin?" she asked.

Tim, who'd been dangling a cat toy on a string for Hot Shot, dropped the string, grabbed up Freddie and ran out of the room.

She stared after him in puzzlement as she listened to Steve.

"Our investigation turned his name up as a Vietnam vet who returned to that country three years ago and brought back to the U.S. a child he claimed was his grandson. Seems he had a birth certificate listing his deceased son as the father. Since the Vietnamese mother was also dead, Martin was allowed to adopt the boy."

"Wait a sec, Steve," she said, understanding now why Tim had run off—he'd heard her repeat his grandfather's name. "You mean Tim's grandfather, Monty Martin, is dead?"

"Murdered, according to the Sacramento cops. Apparently the day before Alice's accident in Nevada."

"Hang on, will you?" She dropped the phone and hurried to find Tim, who didn't respond to her calling his name. Hot Shot, though, unerringly revealed his hiding place under the bed.

She knelt, lifted the spread and peered at Tim. Considering how afraid he was, she chose to be blunt. "Steve just told me your grandfather is dead," she told him. "Monty Martin can't hurt you anymore, so there's no need to hide."

Slowly Tim emerged with Freddie and crawled onto the bed. Hot Shot jumped up to join him.

"I'll be back as soon as I finish talking to Steve," she added. "Okay?"

Tim nodded.

When she picked up the phone again, she asked, "Who killed him? Was it Alice?"

"They aren't sure yet, but they *have* learned Alice's last name—Honders—and contacted the Reno police. If her amnesia is genuine, I don't know how much, if anything, they'll get out of her. I strongly suspect they'll also insist on interviewing Tim. You can't keep him out of this, shrink or not, since it's now a homicide case. I'll keep you posted if I learn anything more before I get there."

"Thanks, Steve." Jade put the phone down and hurried into Tim's room. Sitting on the bed, she put her arm around him, cuddling him next to her.

"Is he really, truly dead?" Tim whispered.

"The Sacramento police say so."

"Then he can't come here and get me."

She hugged him closer. "No. Never."

Later, while Tim was occupied watching his favorite TV program in the family room, she called Gert Severin from the kitchen. After explaining what had happened, Jade asked, "What do you suggest I do if the police insist on talking to Tim? Should you be there?"

"If it's a homicide case, you'll have to allow it. And no, I don't think Tim needs me. If both you and Nathan are present, he should feel secure enough to deal with the questions without too much trauma."

"You think he needs both of us?"

"Definitely. You provide him with the loving mother and Nathan with the protective father. Tim needs all the security he can get."

"Sometimes I think Freddie the Frog provides him with more than either of us," Jade said ruefully.

"Freddie's his talisman and should be there, too. If he seems too upset afterward, bring him by so he and I can have another little talk," Gert advised.

Jade sighed as she hung up. Naturally she intended to keep Tim as secure as possible, even if it meant having to face Nathan again so soon. She would, she supposed, have to call and give him Steve's warning to prepare him ahead of time. First of all, though, she must talk to Tim about what lay ahead.

She waited until his program was over, then sat on the family-room couch. "We're faced with a problem," she told him. "Want to join me while we discuss it?"

Tim climbed up beside her.

Since she thought she had a fair idea of some of the questions the police might ask him, she decided to tell him the truth up front. It was better for him to hear it from her than from a stranger.

"The Sacramento police believe someone killed your grandfather," she said.

He gazed up at her, waiting for more, apparently not shocked or surprised at the news.

"They don't know who killed him so they may come here—or send our local police here—to ask you some questions about the time before Alice took you away from your grandfather's house. If they do, Nathan and I will be there with you.''

He brightened. ''Doc's coming?''

''He will if the police question you.''

''Do I gotta go see Alice?''

''Not unless you change your mind and decide you want to.'' As far as she was concerned, there was no need for the police to force that issue.

''Don't want to.''

''Okay, then.''

''Does Doc know about the police?''

''Not yet. I'm going to call him later, after clinic hours, when he isn't so busy.''

''Can I talk to him? I want to tell him my poem from school.''

Wondering what he meant, Jade nodded, feeling a tad hurt because he hadn't recited any poem to her. Is this how divorced parents felt? Trying not to be upset because their child wanted to share something they knew nothing about with the absent other?

That evening, after she'd explained Steve's call to Nathan and told him what Gert advised, she handed the phone to Tim.

''I made up a poem,'' Tim said, plunging right into it.

Freddie was Laura's
Freddie was Doc's
Freddie is Tim's
Frederick Ferdinand Frog.
He's green.

''Teacher says it's a good poem'n Yasmin likes it.''

Apparently Nathan praised the poem because Tim

grinned happily. They exchanged a few more words before Tim handed the phone back to Jade.

"Let me know if and when the police are coming and I'll be there," Nathan told her.

The call came the next morning. Jade explained that Tim would be back from school by two and they could interview him then. She and his doctor would be present during the questioning. She notified Nathan immediately.

He arrived just as she was pulling in the driveway with Tim. Her watch said it was one-fifteen.

"Any handout for a poor starving man?" he asked.

"Leftovers," she told him.

While Tim toyed with his own sandwich, watching every bite his "Doc" took, Nathan ate cold chicken and warmed-over mashed potatoes with every evidence of enjoyment, finishing off with several oatmeal cookies. She tried not to think about how natural and good it was to see Nathan sitting with Tim in her kitchen, eating food she'd prepared.

"Thanks to you," he said, "Tim and I are now better equipped to face the inquisition—aren't we, cowboy?"

"Yeah," Tim said.

"One thing you got to remember about cops, it's best to tell them the truth right away so they'll stop asking questions and leave you alone. Got that?"

Tim nodded.

"I made up a poem driving here," Nathan said.

Freddie is a frog
He's not a dog.
Hot Shot is a cat
He's not a dirty rat.

"What do you think?"

His answer was a giggle from Tim. Nathan glanced questioningly at Jade.

"It rhymes," she said, glad he was distracting Tim but determined not to be drawn even a millimeter into his web.

Just after two, a Carson deputy arrived with a plainclothes detective from California.

"Does the boy know why we're here, Ms. Adams?" the detective, Lieutenant Soames, asked Jade as she led the way into the living room where Nathan was waiting with Tim.

"I told him his grandfather had been killed," she said, "and that you'd be asking him about it."

After everyone was seated, the lieutenant introduced himself to Nathan and Tim, who sat side by side on the couch. "And this is Deputy Harding," he added.

"Dr. Walker," Nathan said in a level tone, "and Tim. The frog is Freddie."

The lieutenant didn't flicker so much as an eyelash at his introduction to a stuffed toy frog. He leaned forward, focusing on Tim. "Ms. Adams says she told you your grandfather, Monty Martin, had been killed. I'm here to try and find out if you can help me discover who killed him."

Tim stared at him, saying nothing.

"I want you to think about the last time you saw your grandfather," the lieutenant went on. "What was he doing?"

"Yelling at Alice," Tim said.

"What were you doing?"

"Hiding under the bed 'cause I was scared of him."

The lieutenant glanced briefly at the deputy, who was jotting down notes. "What happened next?" he asked.

"He hit Alice. She fell down and he kicked her."

"You could see this from under the bed?"

"Yeah, 'cause they were in the hall."

"So your bedroom door was open?"

Tim nodded.

"Then what happened?"

"He tried to kick Alice some more, but then he fell down. She hit him on the head with something and he didn't get up."

"Did you see what Alice hit him with?"

"Maybe a hammer."

"Was it a hammer?"

Tim hugged Freddie closer. "Yeah."

"What did Alice do then?"

"She pulled me out from under the bed and made me go with her."

"Go with her where?"

"We walked a long time. She found a van and we drove."

"Did Alice say anything to you about what had happened?"

"No."

"Did you ask her?"

"No."

"Did Alice talk to you at all?"

"She said bad words."

"What kind of bad words?"

"Words my teacher told us not to say."

"Did Alice do anything else to your grandfather besides hitting him on the head with the hammer?"

Tim shook his head.

"You're sure."

"Yeah."

"Do you like Alice?"

"No."

"Do you always tell the truth, Tim?"

Tim glanced up at Nathan. "Doc and Jade say I have to. Doc said if I told you the truth, you'd go away. So I did."

The lieutenant couldn't conceal a quickly wiped-off smile. "I can't promise I won't have to come back."

Tim edged closer to Nathan, who put an arm around him.

"The thing is, we need to find out who killed your grandfather," Soames added. "Do you know anything else that might help us?"

After a short silence, Tim shook his head.

Soon after that, the police left.

"Anyone for ice cream?" Nathan asked.

"Me!" Tim cried, then looked at Jade. When she didn't say anything, he answered for her. "Jade likes peach ice cream best'n she puts chocolate on it. But we forgot to buy any when we went shopping. We don't even have vanilla.''

"You go ahead and take Tim," she said to Nathan.

"But you're supposed to come with us," Tim told her.

Unable to resist his pleading look, Jade caved in. "Ice cream, it is."

At least this isn't one-on-one, she consoled herself as the three of them sat in the ice-cream shop.

"Jade took me to a casino," Tim said between licks at his cone. "We had to stand in line, then we got to go to where the food was and I picked out everything I like."

"Buffet," she put in.

"Yeah, buffet. But kids can't go near all those slot machines 'cause they're not like video games. Next Wednesday the teacher's taking us on a field trip. We already went on one to see some baby lambs."

"So what're you going to see this time?" Nathan asked.

"Pet-something. On rocks."

"Petroglyphs," Jade said.

"Yeah, those. Jade's coming to help my teacher. Maybe you can come?"

"I recall you mentioning petroglyphs once," Nathan said to Jade, then turned back to Tim. "If I can get someone to cover for me Wednesday morning, I'll be there, cowboy. Have to meet you at the site, though."

Great, Jade told herself. Another outing with Nathan. Just what she didn't need. Another thought occurred to her and she smiled. "Pat's husband, Rick, will be our fearless leader, so you'll get to meet him. He works part-time as a ranger. We meet at eight-thirty Wednesday morning five miles past Fallon on Highway 50. We hike in from there."

"Ranger Rick, huh? I can see this is an event not to miss."

When Nathan climbed from his Jeep Wednesday morning, he spotted Ranger Rick, in uniform, with a gaggle of kids gathered around him. He also saw Jade, Karen and Pat standing together. Three attractive females, no doubt about it. Why was it, though, his heart lifted only at the sight of Jade?

The day was overcast with a hint of rain in the air but high-desert warm, as was usual in the summer around here. Jade wore khaki shorts and a yellow shirt, her ponytail poking through the back opening of a Northern Nevada Drilling cap. He liked to tease her about being a redhead, but actually her hair was a deep, glowing auburn, as lovely as the rest of her.

He sauntered over, waiting to introduce himself until Rick finished his spiel.

"Glad to have you aboard," Rick said.

"He's my friend," Tim said.

Rick nodded. "Okay, kids, let's get organized. You'll follow me like I told you, by twos, with your assigned buddy. Make your line."

Since there was an even dozen, it worked out with no one left over. Karen's place was after the first three pairs, Jade bringing up the rear, while Pat stayed in front with her husband.

"Hey," Nathan said, falling into place with Jade, "can I be your buddy?"

She shot him a enigmatic but less-than-encouraging glance. "In case you missed the lecture," she said, "we're supposed to remember snakes may be near the rocks and some are poisonous. Rick said a wet year is good for snake reproduction."

"Another thing to blame on the floods," he said. "You know, though, I have yet to see a rattlesnake since I moved to Nevada."

"They do try to stay away from people."

He didn't relish her polite but distant attitude, in place ever since that disastrous night at the ranch when she took it in her head to misunderstand what he was trying to say and wrote him off in royal fashion. He hadn't had a chance to talk to her about it the day Tim was questioned by the cops, but he did need to, and soon.

Phone calls wouldn't work. They needed to get things straightened out face-to-face. Alone. He glanced ahead and, seeing Karen, remembered the thank-you gift Laura had left for him to deliver to Zed and her. That triggered an idea. Why not take advantage of the fact that fate had brought Karen along?

After a time he drifted along the line, talking to Danny and Yasmin, as well as exchanging a few words with Tim. He smiled at Karen.

"Got a problem," he said in a low tone. "Might help if you could offer to take Tim home with you."

She assessed him with a cool blue gaze, then nodded. "You got it."

Back with Jade, he said, "You know, this field trip makes me feel like a parent."

"As far as Tim is concerned, you are."

Maybe so, he told himself, but Mama sure doesn't want to acknowledge me as Daddy.

To keep himself from prematurely bringing up anything personal, he said, "Tell me some more about petroglyphs."

He couldn't decide if Jade looked relieved or not as she answered, "All I know is that they're symbols carved into rock by ancient peoples. Rock paintings, presumably by the same Ancient Ones—the Paiute name for them—are called pictographs. It seems a miracle some still exist after all these years."

Up ahead one of the kids stumbled, fell and let out a wail of pain. Nathan hurried to the little boy, who was wearing shorts, looked at the superficial knee abrasion and asked if anyone had brought along packaged wipes. Pat handed him several and he sponged dirt off the boy's knee, all the while assuring him he was being very brave.

Rick took over, saying the first kid to spot a petroglyph would win a prize. When Yasmin won, Pat handed her a little figurine of a dancing lizard. Rick later pointed out a petroglyph much like the figurine.

Nathan was impressed by the rock art, but what drew the most interest as far as the kids were concerned was the real live lizard that crawled out from between two rocks and scooted off.

After a snack break, it was time to start back. Nathan had just overheard one of the little girls saying, "I liked the baby lambs better," when Rick called an abrupt halt. "Don't anyone move," he warned, pointing to his right. "Look over there."

About ten feet away, a large snake lay coiled in the meager shade of a rocky overhang. In the shadow, Nathan could just make out the faint diamond markings.

Rick took them on a detour around the rattlesnake, but the sight of the reptile was the obvious hit of the field trip and the sole topic of conversation all the way back to Highway 50.

Nathan was beginning to wonder if Karen had changed her mind about helping him when he heard her say to Jade, "We haven't had Tim over for ages. Why don't you let him come home with me?"

With all three kids wildly enthusiastic about the idea, Jade had little choice but to agree, just as Nathan had hoped. She saw Tim off, waving as Karen pulled away, then started for her truck. He intercepted her.

"If I'd known Karen would be here today," he said, "I'd have brought Laura's gift with me to give to her. It's too big to mail and sort of perishable, and unfortunately I don't know when I'll get the chance to go by the ranch. Since you're a regular visitor there, I'd appreciate it if you'd stop by the clinic, pick up the gift and deliver it for me. Now's as good a time as any for me."

He thought Jade eyed him with as much mistrust as she had the rattlesnake. "We're not anywhere near Tourmaline," she objected.

Careful to seem indifferent, he shrugged. "If you don't have time, no problem. Maybe Karen or Zeb can drop by sometime and pick it up." He watched to see how she'd deal with the guilt trip he was trying to lay on her.

Pat finally got the rest of the kids loaded into her big van and tooted as she drove off. Rick's truck sped after her. He waved.

"Nice couple," Nathan said, waving back.

"Yes, they are." Jade sounded annoyed. "I suppose I don't have any choice but to follow you to the clinic."

"Laura didn't mean to cause anyone trouble," he said, keeping up the pressure.

"Will you stop that!" she snapped. "I said I'd come."

He tried his best to look innocent of any hidden agenda. "Thanks. See you there."

Jade's pickup was close behind him when he pulled into the clinic parking lot. He glanced at his watch as he got out of the Jeep. Eleven. He had an hour of free time left.

"It's on the screened porch," he told her. "We can go around the back."

They went through the gate and walked together across the grass. "I see you took the badminton net down," she said.

"My lawn service needed to cut the grass." He curbed his impatience to get beyond polite conversation. Not quite yet.

He opened the screen door for her and she stepped

inside. "Whoa!" she exclaimed, staring at Laura's gift.

He, too, gazed at the large tub containing a good-size dwarf lemon tree, blossoming at the moment. "I gather Laura was prompted by something Karen said about wishing she could grow her own lemons, but Carson Valley was too cold. This is supposed to thrive indoors."

Jade took a deep breath and smiled. "Citrus blossoms always smell so wonderful."

"Strange the scent is so sweet when lemons are so sour. And speaking of sour..." He paused. "Please sit down. I have a few things that need to be said."

She eyed him, frowning, making him believe she'd refuse. Short of forcing her into a chair and hog-tying her, he had no way to keep her here except by words.

"As a favor to me, Jade," he added.

Finally she shrugged and sat on the wooden swing. He remained standing, searching for the right words. It had been simpler to get her here than to find a way to make her understand how he saw their relationship.

"The last thing I intended to do that night at the ranch was to drive you away," he said finally. "You and I, we're like a team— No, that's not what I mean. More like partners. Not just because of Tim but because we mesh well."

He sat beside her on the swing and took her hand, absently stroking her fingers as he continued, "I can't deny wanting you—you're in my blood."

She stared at him, her lips slightly parted, and it

was all he could do not to lean over and kiss her. Not yet. Maybe not at all for now.

"What I was trying to say the other night was I can't promise you anything permanent. It wasn't fair to go on without telling you that."

"Laura already told me," she said.

It was his turn to stare. "Laura?"

"We liked each other right away. I think that's why she warned me not to get too attached to you."

He couldn't judge how she felt about all this, but at least she hadn't jumped up and rushed off. Laura's warning to her had taken him by surprise, making him unsure how to go on. Whatever had gotten into his sister?

"Anyway, I knew from the beginning whatever was between us wouldn't last." Jade's voice held the hint of a tremor, telling him she wasn't as calm as she appeared on the surface.

"Just because that's true doesn't mean we have to break off abruptly," he said, belatedly hearing the desperate edge to his words. He didn't want to lose her, couldn't bear to think about it.

"I disagree. In the long run we both—"

He'd gone past being able to reason with himself. He wanted, he needed...

Pulling her to him roughly, he covered her mouth with his, cutting off the words he didn't care to hear, his kiss demanding a response. For one endless, awful moment her lips lay lifeless under his. He was about to let her go when she came alive in his arms.

His heart leaped with joy when she started to return his kiss with passionate fervor, becoming his

Jade once again. His desire fueled anew, he deepened the kiss, tasting her sweetness, reveling in her eager response.

Knowing her, it was entirely possible he hadn't really won, but at least he'd made her admit she needed him, too. You might call it a compromise—something rare for her.

Chapter Fourteen

Jade had been on edge the entire morning, anticipating Nathan's arrival at the site, then fighting to stay cool and distant when he got there. Her defenses held until she reached the clinic, but then began to collapse when they got to the screened porch and he sat down next her on the swing, taking her hand. One by one the walls fell as his fingers played with hers. When he finally caught her to him and kissed her, only token resistance remained.

Knowing she was where she belonged, in Nathan's arms, Jade couldn't help but indulge her need to be there. The swing beneath them swayed back and forth as their embrace grew more fevered and they shifted position to hold each other closer.

Desire enveloped her, heating mind and body, narrowing her world down to just him, all time collapsed into now. His soft murmur of her name against her lips mingled with the creak of the swing to become erotic love music.

Breathing in his scent with the sweet perfume of lemon blossoms seemed a heady, though unneeded, aphrodisiac. The motion of the swing grew more erratic until he stood, pulling her to her feet with him, cupping her against him. If only they had forever to be together like this.

Forever. The word echoed uncomfortably in her mind, allowing snippets of reality in.

With Nathan there was no forever, no kind of permanence. With him there was only now and maybe tomorrow, possibly next week. Is that what she wanted? Because it was all she could count on.

Never mind, her body urged. Seize the now.

But the spell was broken. Aching with unfulfilled need, she extricated herself from their embrace. When she tried to speak, her throat closed.

"Jade," he said huskily, "what's wrong?"

Forcing words out, she said, "Nowhere. Us."

"Nowhere?"

"To go, I mean." Words began to come easier. "Better to give it up while we still like each other and can be friends for Tim's sake. I don't want to get into what my drilling crews call a do-over."

"You're not making sense."

She took a moment to gather the right words. "Sometimes, no matter how careful the crew is, a cave-in occurs. When that happens, all your time and whatever pipe and other equipment you've used is lost, and there's nothing that can be done about it. Everything's gone. The well has to be done over.

"I'm afraid that's what will happen with us, and we'll lose whatever feeling we have for each other. New wells can be dug, but human relationships often can't be reconstructed. And remember, we have more than ourselves to think about. If ours caves in, what about Tim, who needs us both?"

"You're overreacting." Annoyance tinged his words. "In my opinion we can go on as we are indefinitely."

Jade shook her head. "You're wrong. What's between us is too…" She paused, eliminating "strong" as the chosen word, groping for another. "It's too acute," she said at last. "Like a possibly fatal disease."

"Come on, Jade—neither of us is in any danger of expiring."

"You're refusing to understand the point."

"Because I don't see it."

She resisted the impulse to stamp her foot like a frustrated child. Why was he being so obtuse? "You began this discussion back at the ranch in the moonlight. All I'm doing is continuing it. Didn't you use the words 'draw back'? Well, that's exactly what I'm doing."

She watched his fists clench and relax as he spoke. "I meant we should step back a tad and discuss the fact that marriage can't come into the picture. Just so we both knew where we stand."

"I know exactly where we stand. Not only no marriage, no permanence, either. Marriage doesn't hap-

pen to be on my agenda, but a day-to-day relationship doesn't appeal to me in the slightest." Turning
away from him, she headed for the screen door.

His hand clamped down on her shoulder, halting
her. "Nothing was said about day-to-day, dammit. I
recognize what's between us is no one-night stand."

She jerked free. "I'm finished with the discussion." Before he could move, she opened the door
and went out.

He'd started to follow her when, to her relief, she
heard his buzzer go off. Hurrying through the back
gate, she climbed into the pickup. Only after she was
barreling down the narrow road did she realize she'd
left the damn lemon tree behind. Inexplicably that
made her burst into tears.

She slowed, easing onto the shoulder and stopping
until the worst was over, angry at herself for crying
and also for feeling she'd lost something precious
beyond recall.

Nathan pulled himself together enough to begin
seeing patients. The familiar routine gradually
calmed him, but a heavy nugget of loss remained.
Why did he have to get mixed up with a woman who
couldn't compromise?

Once the clinic closed for the day and he was in
his apartment, he found himself pacing the living
room. The image of a caged hamster came to him
and he stopped abruptly, disgusted. A hamster of all
things. Hell, why couldn't he have imagined himself
a caged tiger?

The hamster was Tim's influence, no doubt. That

was the only thing Jade was right about—they did have to remember Tim. But each of them being there for the boy had nothing to do with their relationship. Friends, she'd said. As if what they had could be reduced to a sexually neutral state.

He'd never felt for any woman, including Gloria, what he felt for Jade. It wasn't simply infatuation; with Gloria he'd learned all about how quickly that state faded. Maybe the word he sought was…love?

Sinking onto the couch, he tried to come to terms with the fact he might have—no, dammit, had—fallen in love with a woman he absolutely didn't want to marry.

And to cap it off, he still hadn't gotten rid of Laura's lemon-tree gift.

In the days that followed, Jade tried not to mope around because that upset Tim. Even Hot Shot seemed to sense her sad state because he followed her about the house, uttering questioning meows.

"Hot Shot misses Doc," Tim told her, which did nothing to lighten her mood.

When Karen called to tell her Steve had arrived and wanted Tim, Nathan and her to come to the ranch on Sunday, she snapped, "You'll have to call Nathan, because I'm not going to."

"Another spat?" Karen asked.

"I just don't care to talk to him, that's all."

"I recognize the symptoms. Been there, done that."

"It's not the same as you and Zed before you got

married," Jade insisted. "Not the same at all. For one thing, Nathan and I will never marry."

"If you say so. Whatever. I'll take care of getting Nathan here."

When Jade pulled the pickup to a stop at the ranch on Sunday, Zed and Nathan were wrestling the lemon tree out of the Jeep onto a small hand-pulled truck.

"I could wish your sister wasn't quite so thoughtful," Zed was saying.

"The guy from the Tourmaline nursery who delivered it to the clinic felt the same way," Nathan told him.

"Karen will be pleased, though," Jade put in.

Tim stayed to watch the men, leaving her to walk to the house alone. Steve rose from a chair in the patio and hugged her. "Seems like a long time since I hugged you last," he said.

"I can't believe you're getting sentimental," she told him. "That's not the Steve I know."

"Came on me suddenly. There's something about family..." He let his words trail off.

She eyed him appraisingly and he shrugged. "It won't last. Come on inside. Karen and Linnea have enough food stacked up to last us a week."

Once in the house, she discovered Karen had gone to the addition to show Zed and Nathan where she wanted the lemon tree placed.

"You look as tired as Steve did when he got here," Linnea said. "Trouble with the drilling?"

Jade shook her head with some reluctance, knowing what was coming next.

"That leaves men," Linnea said. "I know the feeling."

Everyone seemed to know the feeling and yet none of them possibly could. Linnea was as happily married to Talal as Karen was to Zed. Not that she believed marriage cured all ills, but, dammit, they were happy.

"Karen wants us to come to the family room in the addition so we can admire the lemon tree while we have refreshments," Linnea said. "Jade, if you'll push the serving cart and Steve carries this extra tray of stuff, we'll be all set."

When they reached the family room, the lemon tree was looking good in its new home near the floor-to-ceiling windows overlooking the flower garden and the pond beyond.

Tim hadn't come in with the men, so Jade knew he'd found Danny and Yasmin to play with.

"The perfect spot for the tree," Karen said to Nathan. "You have a delightful sister. Be sure you give me Laura's address so I can thank her properly for a most insightful gift. Now, everybody, pour yourself whatever, sit down and nibble so we can listen to Steve before the wild trio descends on us or Erin wakes up from her nap."

"Karen told me the cops questioned Tim," Steve began, "and that he said he saw Alice hit his grandfather over the head with a hammer in the hall outside his bedroom. As it turns out, her blows did result in a skull fracture, but that wasn't the cause of death.''

"You mean Alice didn't kill him?'' Jade asked in surprise.

Steve held up a hand. "Wait. Martin was found dead in the kitchen, not the hall. He'd been garroted but not before he put up a struggle.''

Jade glanced at Nathan, who raised his eyebrows at her. If not Alice, who?

"A neighbor down the block, who'd been walking his dog, claims he saw two people run out of Martin's house and get into a large dark-colored van. The neighbor insisted he'd seen Tim and Alice often enough to know it wasn't them.''

"The Vietnamese couple!'' Jade exclaimed. "The ones who tried to take Tim away from me.''

Steve nodded. "The woman was released from the Reno hospital, but the man's still recuperating there. He wasn't cooperative with the cops, but through an interpreter, they questioned his wife and she talked. The man turns out to be Tim's uncle, his dead mother's brother. According to the woman's story, she was deliberately left behind in Vietnam when her husband, Tim's uncle, came to this country—the reason being that Tim's mother was dying and she was supposed to bring Tim with her to the U.S. when the death actually occurred.''

"Then Tim must have seen her there and that's why he thought he might know her,'' Jade said.

"The woman still resents being left behind, which may be why she spilled the beans to the cops. In any case, Martin showed up and whisked Tim off before she could do her part. When she arrived alone, her husband was furious and beat her. From then on he nourished a deadly hatred for Monty Martin, who'd made him violate his promise to his dying sister."

Steve took a swallow of his drink, set it down and continued, "It took him a couple of years to locate Martin. Whether he'd had the house staked out or not, I didn't learn, but apparently he arrived that night after Tim and Alice ran off. Martin had revived enough to get to the kitchen. When Tim's uncle burst in demanding he turn over Tim, Martin went for him. According to the wife, Martin was not the first man her husband had killed."

"Tim's uncle will stand trial for murder, I take it," Nathan said.

"At least. The FBI is interested in him, too, so there may be other charges."

"Then there's no chance he'll be able to claim Tim?"

"None. As far as we could determine, the boy has no other living relatives." He glanced from Nathan to Jade. "The ball's in your court as far as Tim is concerned."

"Alice is no relation at all?" Jade asked, wanting to be sure.

"No. Once they knew her last name, they located a sister who came to take Alice home with her. She told them Alice had been living with Martin less than a year. Since there was no reason to press charges against Alice except for the van stolen in California, the police allowed her to go back there with her sister."

"Jade and I need to confer," Nathan said, rising. He held out a hand to help her up, and seeing no reason not to, she took it, allowing him to lead her outside and into the gazebo.

A giant cottonwood spread thick branches over the gazebo roof, keeping the sun away, and as usual, the wind blew, so it wasn't unbearably hot there. Jade tucked a stray strand of hair behind her ear and said, "Well?"

"We don't have a choice," he said. "I've looked at it from all angles and made my decision. Since you're friendly with local judges, you might possibly be allowed to adopt Tim as a single parent. That's not fair to him, though—he needs a father. I'm not cut out to be a part-time parent. I love the kid and I want to help raise him—full-time."

Jade wasn't any too sure where this was leading. Did he mean to insist they live together? No way. She was opening her mouth to say so when he spoke again.

"There's no other alternative. We'll have to get married."

Jade stared at him in utter disbelief, finally managing to blurt out, "But you don't want to get married."

"What's that got to do with anything? We're talking about Tim here and what's best for him."

"No!" She all but shouted the word. "I refuse to marry you."

His initially astonished expression gave way to anger. "Why? Am I that repulsive?"

"Marriage is out. If you insist on being Tim's father, fine. I agree he needs one and he prefers you. I'm almost sure I can adopt him the way you said— as a single parent. I want you to consider this—many divorced parents raise children, sharing their upbringing. Why can't we share Tim?''

Nathan's voice rose. ''Are you serious? Of all the crackpot suggestions, yours wins the prize. I want Tim to be my son, to live with us both—and all you suggest is divorce.''

''We can't get divorced—we're not married.''

''Only because you won't listen to reason.''

They glared at each other.

Impasse, Jade thought. She didn't intend to give so much as a millimeter, either. How could she be expected to agree to marry a man who didn't want her for a wife but just as a mother for the boy they both loved? She could and would be that mother without his great sacrifice, thank you.

Deadlock, thanks to her mind-set against compromise, Nathan told himself. Why was she so upset about getting married? Hell, she was the one who'd mentioned permanence.

Both heard the sliding door to the family room open and close. They turned to look at Steve, coming toward the gazebo.

''There's a call for you, Nathan,'' Steve said. ''A Dr. Severin.''

Although he wasn't taking calls this Sunday, Nathan had left Zed's number with his answering service. Gert wouldn't be bothering him unless she had an emergency, and he did owe her. Concentrating on what Gert might want, he strode from the gazebo without a word and entered the house.

"You both got pretty loud," Steve told Jade. "We couldn't help overhearing some of your argument."

"He's totally unreasonable," she muttered. "How could he possibly imagine I'd want a martyr for a husband?"

Steve shrugged. "I did what I could for you guys concerning Tim. The rest is up to you."

Belatedly recalling Steve's reluctance to deal with emotion, Jade curbed her impulse to tell him everything she was feeling.

"Thanks," she managed to say. "I appreciate the trouble you went to."

By the time she and Steve reentered the family room, there was no sign of Nathan.

"He said it was an emergency," Zed told her.

Jade knew that whatever had called him away, he wouldn't be back. Aware everyone in the room had heard at least part of her disagreement with Nathan, she expected to be fending off questions she didn't want to answer. Instead, Zed urged Talal to tell Steve the problems he was having with the contractor building his house. Talal complied with what seemed suspicious eagerness.

I embarrassed them, Jade told herself, then shook her head. Her family wasn't easily embarrassed. Were they upset with her? No, any and all of them would be quick to tell her if they were. What, then? Why were they deliberately steering clear of what they'd overheard?

Heaven only knows, every last one of them, even

Steve, was the curious type. Yet nobody asked her one single question.

In counterpart to the men dissing the contractor, Karen and Linnea got into a totally boring discussion of the best way to cook lamb, with garlic or rosemary or with both, which was unlike either of them. They'd never been the sort to exchange recipes.

When Jade heard the first faint whimpers coming down the hall from Erin's room, she sprang to her feet, saying, "I'll get her." She fled with relief from what was beginning to seem like a bunch of strangers.

She changed Erin's diapers, then stopped her fussing by playing finger games with her, all the while controlling the hurt inside, not allowing it to take control.

"Tee," Erin crowed, and she hugged the little girl to her until Erin squeaked in protest.

Taking a deep breath, she left the room, bringing Erin to her mother. Her happily married mother. But when she got there, Erin held out her arms to Zed, instead, saying "Daddy." Her happily married father reached for her, smiling.

Yasmin had come in while Jade was busy in Erin's room and now sat on the couch between Talal and Linnea, bent over whispering to the baby inside her mother. "I'll love you right away," she was saying. "As soon as you come out, even if I can't play with you till you get bigger."

Here was a loving, married father and mother with the baby-to-come also blessed with a loving little sister.

Jade closed her eyes momentarily, aware no one was doing any of this on purpose. Still, she could hardly bear it.

Was her attitude fair to Tim? she wondered. She loved Nathan, misguided though he was, loved him past reason. Did he love her? Wouldn't he have told her so if he did? She sighed. How could either of them be happy in a marriage he didn't, in his heart of hearts, want?

Feeling miserable, she decided she'd had enough of her all-too-happy family and wanted to go home. "It's time I left," she said abruptly. "I'll go collect Tim and—"

"Oh, you can't do that," Karen cut in. "Yasmin just told us he and Danny are off on the ponies with Moe. You wouldn't want to cut his ride short."

Moe, Jade knew, was one of her brother's hired hands. And no, she didn't want to spoil Tim's fun.

"Besides," Linnea put in, "we planned a special supper for you and Tim."

It wouldn't be fair to disappoint her sisters-in-law, either, after they'd gone to the trouble of fixing the meal with Tim and her in mind.

"I think I'll take a walk around the place, then," she said, feeling a desperate need to be by herself.

Yasmin sprang up. "We got baby pigs," she said. "Come and see." She held out her hand.

Apparently she was doomed not to be left alone, Jade thought as she allowed Yasmin to lead her past the barn toward the pigpen. She tried not to hear the child's chatter about what the coming baby's name might be, but some of it got through to her.

"...Ellen for a girl, Shas for a boy. Mama says it's a good thing she has time to get used to that Shas name."

"Shas was my father's name," Jade said slowly, shaken from her preoccupation with her own misery. "He was Zed and Talal's father, too. And Ellen was our mother."

Yasmin blinked, obviously trying to puzzle out how three grown people could all have the same father and mother.

"You're luckier than we were," Jade went on. "You know your father and mother. Zed and Talal and I were raised by our grandparents because our father, Shas, and our mother, Ellen, died."

"I'm lucky," Yasmin repeated with her sweet, charming smile.

Jade knelt and hugged her. Yasmin was luckier than she knew to have been adopted by Talal and Linnea and loved as much as if she'd been born to them.

"And hey, they're pretty lucky to be raising a smart little daughter like you," she told the girl.

"Tim said you were gonna be his mama," Yasmin said. "And Doc was gonna be his daddy."

Jade nodded, glad to see the pigpen in front of them so she could change the subject to piglets. She'd had it up to here with happy families and mamas and daddies.

Chapter Fifteen

Though for Jade, the time seemed endless, eventually the supper hour rolled around. To keep busy and avoid conversation, she fed Erin beforehand, then helped Yasmin entertain her while Karen and Linnea took care of the final meal preparations.

Danny and Tim had come in earlier to join the men watching a game on TV.

Jade was just handing Yasmin the little silver bell that was always rung to summon everyone to a meal when a knock sounded at the back door.

"Get that, would you, Jade?" Karen asked.

Jade crossed to the door, opened it and stood there gaping at Nathan. What was he doing back here?

"I was invited, honest," he told her.

"But you had an emergency."

"Most don't take forever. Karen and Zed insisted I return when I could, so I did."

Belatedly realizing she was blocking his entry, Jade moved aside.

The silver bell tinkled.

"Arriving just in time to eat, apparently," Nathan added, easing past her.

In the dining room, Jade noticed what she hadn't paid attention to before—a place had already been set for Nathan. She'd had no idea he might come back.

"Look at all the rice!" Tim said excitedly after taking his place.

Linnea hadn't been exaggerating when she'd said the meal had been planned for Jade and Tim. There were three kinds of rice dishes—all favorites of Tim's. And Karen had made her special chicken pot pie, which she knew Jade loved.

Unfortunately Jade's appetite had gone on vacation. How could she be expected to enjoy the meal with Nathan sitting directly across from her? She couldn't even look up without encountering that blue gaze of his. A vagrant thought breezed past—Italian blue? Damn. She didn't care anymore, so why keep trying to place the exact color?

"How good it is to have the family together," Talal said. "I hope to persuade Grandmother Noorah to come from Kholi for a visit when our house is finished. I know she's eager to meet Jaida, the grand-daughter she's never seen. And become reacquainted with Zeid, as well."

"And meet me, too," Danny said. "'N Erin."

Talal nodded. "Perhaps others, as well." He exchanged a glance with Zed.

Jade looked from one to the other of them suspiciously. Were they up to something? "Who else?" she demanded.

"Must be me," Steve said, grinning. "I'm a bona fide in-law, after all."

So he was.

Linnea laid a hand on her swollen abdomen. "And there's this one, too."

Jade managed a smile for her.

The meal dragged on, Jade pushing food around her plate as she tried to pretend she was eating. In her entire life, never before had any man made her lose her appetite. At any moment she expected one of her relatives to notice and want to know what was wrong.

She didn't contribute to the general conversation, either, and noticed Nathan was quiet, too. Perhaps because Tim, sitting next to him, was regaling him with a blow-by-blow account of the pony ride.

The death of Tim's grandfather hadn't seemed to upset the boy. Then again, why should he be sorry the man who'd been so brutal to him had died? As for her, she could feel no emotion other than relief that Tim was safe now.

And would continue to be. With her. To be fair to the boy, she'd work out some kind of arrangement where Tim could spend time with Nathan.

"Who, me?" Steve's question made her realize she'd lost track of what was being said or who was saying it.

"No way," he continued. "One time at bat was enough for me. I've given up the marriage game for good. It's not the only game in town, after all."

"I hope some day to see you eat those words, dear brother," Karen told him.

Steve shook his head, smiling.

Jade couldn't help but glance at Nathan and found he was gazing directly at her. Or perhaps "glaring" was a more accurate choice of word. She looked away.

"Never say never," Talal put in. "Look at me."

"And me," Linnea added. "Here you see two marriage-shy doubters who had to eat their words."

Talal touched her cheek with the back of his hand. "Very tasty they were."

Jade frowned. Was all this talk of marriage deliberate, or was she being paranoid?

"When I grow up I'm gonna marry Yasmin," Tim said.

His announcement made everyone smile except Danny and Yasmin.

"You got to ask me first," Yasmin said, "'N' I might say no."

Danny looked from Yasmin to Tim and back. "*I'm* gonna marry Yasmin," he stated in no uncertain terms.

Yasmin raised her chin. "Maybe I don't wanna get married," she announced. "Maybe you got to go ask another girl."

Erin, her high chair pulled up to the table, banged her cup on the tray, obviously tired of being ignored. "Me!" she cried. "Me!"

Kids and all laughed.

The dessert turned out to be peach ice cream with hot-fudge topping. Since she knew it was for her and wouldn't offend Karen for the world, Jade forced herself to choke down most of her serving somehow.

The kids excused themselves, making Erin set up a clamor to get down.

"Children in the family room for a brand-new Disney video, adults in the living room," Karen announced. "We'll leave the cleanup till later. Zed, please bring the playpen from the patio and put it in the family room where Erin can watch the video with the others."

Jade didn't care to join her family in the living room, so she said to Karen, "I can start the cleanup now while you guys are—"

"Absolutely not." Although Karen used her teacher's voice seldom, when she did no one disobeyed her. Jade was no exception, so she sighed and wandered into the living room.

Talal waved her toward a seat on the two-person settee where Nathan was already. When she tried to veer aside, Talal took her arm and saying, "Indulge me, please, sister of mine," led her to the settee.

She was no stranger to scenes, but she didn't feel like creating one this evening. So she sat next to Nathan, careful not to touch him. But she was far from cowed.

"Since when do we have assigned seats?" she demanded.

"Zeid and I have arranged a presentation for everyone," Talal said, "and the seating is crucial."

When everyone was in place, Talal said, "Some of you here were present a few years back, at a time when Erin was not so much as an idea. To be exact, my brother, Zeid, my sister, Jaida, and my not-yet sister-in-law, Karen. Danny, no more than a baby, was with us, but since he would have no memory of the occasion, he's been excluded."

Jade watched her brother through narrowed eyes. What was he getting at?

"Steve, you, Nathan and Linnea are guests, living this for the first time while the rest of us relive what happened." Talal paused and glanced around the room. "Nathan, however, will also be a participant."

Zed said, "Imagine the time as shortly before Karen and I were to be married—for all the wrong reasons, or so we both believed. Talal had the wits to see this and to do something to alter it. I'd confessed to him my deep love for my reluctant bride, so when we were all gathered in this room, he asked if I'd ever thought to tell Karen how I felt."

"He hadn't, of course," Karen put in.

"But with my brother's urging, I blurted it out then and there," Zed admitted.

"Then Talal turned on me," Karen said, "and asked me the same question—did I love Zed and had I ever told him so?"

Zed smiled at her. "She'd kept it a well-concealed secret."

Karen took his hand. "It was secret no more, after that."

Talal looked at Jade. "You were a witness. Do you remember the occasion?"

Apprehension choked her, but she managed to mumble, "Yes." What was all this in aid of?

Talal focused on Nathan. "As unwitting eavesdroppers, we all heard you propose marriage to Jaida earlier today. Why did you? You must think about what your real reason was before you answer."

She felt Nathan tense beside her and opened her mouth to protest.

Talal forestalled her. "Jaida, are you willing to uphold what is now a family tradition, or do you intend to go on being your usual argumentative self? Pride can sometimes be a virtue, but more often it closes doors. You refused Nathan's offer. He will now make it again and you must scuttle that troublesome Zohir pride and answer him honestly."

All eyes focused on Nathan, but he, turning to Jade, looked only at her. She saw him swallow convulsively.

"I love you," he said hoarsely. "It's been a long incubation period, but the bug finally conquered me. I'm in love with what may be the stubbornnest woman in Nevada, maybe the entire country, and there's no way I'm ever going to get over it." He took her hand. "Will you marry me, Jade?"

Almost too overcome to speak, she fumbled for words. "I...you..." Getting hold of herself, she said, "And you think *I'm* stubborn? Why didn't you tell me that in the first place? I've probably been in love with you from the moment you first stepped out of that red Jeep with its crazy snowplow attachment, only I wouldn't admit it to myself until lately. Of course I'll marry you."

She looked away from him, her gaze traveling over her jubilant relatives. "In fact, maybe we'd better elope right now."

As Nathan pulled her into his arms and kissed her, she heard Karen say, "Not on your life, girl. You planned my wedding—now it's my turn."

Then Jade was caught up in the wonder and passion of the love they shared and there was no one but Nathan.

They were married in September, close to Linnea's due date, so she made a very pregnant matron-of-honor, sharing the the responsibility with Karen. Surrounded by her family, Jade felt a renewed closeness to them all.

Yet she knew when she walked up the aisle, flanked by her twin brothers who would be giving her away, that she'd renounce the entire world for the man who waited for her at the altar. Love struck when you least expected it, and when it did, it was for keeps.

Tim, the proud ring bearer, kept his cool until after the ceremony ended and the groom was told he might kiss the bride. At this point, Tim faced the guests and announced proudly, "That's my mama and daddy kissing."

Which they would legally be very soon.

At the reception Laura took Jade aside. "I'm so happy Nathan came to his senses," she said. "I knew as soon as I met you that you were right for him, and I was so afraid he wouldn't let go of his bitterness. I hope you'll forgive me for telling you he'd never marry again. How glad I am to be wrong!''

"I'm as glad as you are that you were wrong," Jade told her. "And I hope now that your brother has shown you the way, you'll give some thought to giving marriage a try."

Laura's smile faded and she shook her head. "I don't think so."

Someone else came up before Jade could continue her conversation with her new sister-in-law, and in the flurry of congratulations and wishes for happiness, she forgot about Laura.

Later she heard Karen teasing her brother, saying if Nathan had the guts to stand up to bat again, why didn't Steve consider giving the marriage game a second chance?

"I can't imagine any circumstance where I'd be willing to marry again," Steve told her. "Give it a rest, sis." He turned to Jade, asking, "So where are you going to live? I understand it posed a problem."

"Gert—she's a colleague of Nathan's—found us the perfect house in Tourmaline. It's an old Victorian in need of TLC but livable while we're having it returned to its glory days. Nathan and I adore the house and so does Tim—he and the cat enjoy all those funny little nooks and crannies."

"How about that fantastic place of yours up at the lake?"

"I'm keeping it for now. A friend of Zed's will be renting it for the next year while he builds along the lake, then we'll see."

"I almost envy you," Steve said. "But not enough to get caught in the trap myself."

When Steve moved on, Tim said to her, "What did he mean about a trap?"

"He said that because he doesn't understand," she told Tim. "You and I and Nathan know the truth."

"About what?"

"About love, silly."

"Oh, yeah—that."

Jade smiled as Nathan appeared. He ruffled Tim's hair and put an arm around her.

She looked up into her husband's eyes, more blue than the Nevada sky, and said, "Remember the time you refused to write a prescription for me because you knew it wasn't necessary? What if I asked you for an unwritten one now, a prescription for happiness?"

He brushed his fingers over her lips. "Any doctor worthy of the name knows that love is the best medicine to guarantee being happy. And, hey, we got that already."

* * * * *

SILHOUETTE
SPECIAL EDITION®

AVAILABLE FROM 19TH MAY 2000

SHE'S HAVING HIS BABY Linda Randall Wisdom

That's My Baby!

Jake Roberts was everything Caitlin O'Hara wanted in her baby's father—he was fun, warm and gorgeous. They'd shared every intimate detail of their lives since childhood. Why not a baby?

A FATHER'S VOW Myrna Temte

Montana

Sam Brightwater wanted to start a traditional family. So the *last* woman he should be attracted to was Julia Stedman, who was only sampling her heritage. But Julia got under his skin and soon they were making love and making a baby...

BETH AND THE BACHELOR Susan Mallery

Beth was a suburban mother of two and her friends had set her up with a blind date—millionaire bachelor Todd Graham! He was sexy, eligible—everything a woman could want...

BUCHANAN'S PRIDE Pamela Toth

Leah Randall took in the man without a memory, but she had no idea who he was. They never planned to fall in love, not when he could be anyone...even one of her powerful Buchanan neighbours!

THE LONG WAY HOME Cheryl Reavis

Rita Warren had come home. She had things to prove. She didn't need a troublemaking soldier in her already complicated life. But 'Mac' McGraw was just impossible to ignore.

CHILD MOST WANTED Carole Halston

Susan Gulley had become a mother to her precious orphaned nephew, but she hadn't banked on falling for his handsome but hard-edged uncle. What would Jonah do when he learned the secret she'd been keeping?

Welcome back to the drama and mystery that is the Fortune Dynasty.

A Fortune's Children Wedding is coming to you at a special price of only £3.99 and contains a money off coupon for issue one of *Fortune's Children Brides*.

With issue one priced at a special introductory offer of 99p you can get it **FREE** with your money off coupon.

Sometimes bringing up baby can bring surprises –and showers of love! For the cutest and cuddliest heroes and heroines, choose the Special Edition™ book marked

That's my baby!

SILHOUETTE
SPECIAL EDITION®

TMB/RTL1